Paxton

FARRADAY COUNTRY ∾ BOOK SIXTEEN

CHRIS KENISTON

Indie House Publishing

Indie House Publishing

MORE BOOKS

By Chris Keniston

The Billionaire Barons of Texas

Just One Date
Just One Spark
Just One Dance
Just One Take
Just One Taste
Just One Shot
Just One Chance
Just One Mistake
Just One Family
Just One Rodeo
Just One Surprise
Just One Look

Hart Land

Heather
Lily
Violet
Iris
Hyacinth
Rose
Calytrix
Zinnia
Poppy
Picture Perfect

Farraday Country

Adam
Brooks
Connor
Declan
Ethan
Finn

Grace
Hannah
Ian
Jamison
Keeping Eileen
Loving Chloe
Morgan
Neil
Owen
Paxton
Quinn

Honeymoon Series
Honeymoon for One
Honeymoon for Three
Honeymoon for Four
Honeymoon for Five
Honeymoon for Six
Honeymoon for Seven

Aloha Romance Series:
Aloha Texas
Almost Paradise
Mai Tai Marriage
Dive Into You
Look of Love
Love by Design
Love Walks In
Shell Game
Flirting with Paradise

Surf's Up Flirts:
(Aloha Series Companions)
Shall We Dance
Love on Tap
Head Over Heels
Perfect Match
Just One Kiss
It Had to Be You
Cat's Meow

CHAPTER ONE

"**A**nd... cut."

Now that the cameras weren't running, Paxton Farraday leaned left then right, stretching out his back. Even though he'd argued there was no need to film replacing the hotel bathroom when that episode was already over and in the can, what the production company wanted, the production company got. Still, it was bad enough he was feeling his last birthday, there was no reason to record his aching back on camera for the world to see.

"I hate bathtub installs." Quinn, Paxton's next older brother—not including the five-minute Owen had on him—rolled his shoulders. Apparently, he wasn't the only one with age troubles. "Single tub isn't so bad but these blasted all-in-one units have a mind of their own."

"Yeah, remind me never to complain about hauling bags of mulch or root ball trees again. Lugging and installing bathtubs is modern day torture." He cracked his back. "It's downright painful."

"Agreed." Quinn nodded. "Next time the younger guys can haul these things around."

The camera crew pulled back. Someone shouted lunch break and standing in the doorway, sporting a floppy hat, and big sunglass—the only carryover from her fashionable days in Los Angeles—Valerie, Morgan's wife and the show's producer, rushed up to them. "Excellent shoot, guys. Executive feedback on the last few episodes has been great and the internet buzz with the fan base is, well, buzzing. Now, we need to talk about that off-camera build."

Paxton exchanged a glance with Quinn. "Off-camera build?"

Her gaze narrowing, his brother Morgan's wife dropped her hands on her hips. "Don't you two read any of my memos?"

"Of course we do." Frowning, Quinn spoke up before Paxton could admit he might skim a few.

Even though Valerie was smiling, her frustration with her brothers-in-law was apparent. "The show was approached to sponsor a new home build for a needy family. Since the ratings were so high for the homestead fixer-upper, the execs thought a similar project for charity would be fabulous publicity. They were on it like white on rice."

Now that he thought about it, Paxton remembered noticing the name of a well-known charity in one of her never-ending memos, but had skimmed more than usual. "Must have missed the details on that one, but, of course, you know we're game to help. Within reason."

Quinn nodded. "Agreed. But off camera? How is that going to boost ratings for the show?"

"There might be a camera crew once in a while for social media reels. Now that we've just about finished this season, once we film the wrap-up episode, you guys will have plenty of time on your hands for the project."

Plenty of time? Paxton didn't mind helping out anyone going through a rough patch, but the construction company had projects lined up for the season break from here to Oklahoma and back. "We'd better find Owen, but can we discuss this somewhere other than this cramped bathroom?"

Valerie looked around and chuckled. "Good point. Let's go outside."

Paxton followed her with Quinn on his heels. They settled at a picnic table by Molly's food truck.

Setting her insulated mug on the table, Valerie looked from one brother to the other. "The build is a standard three bed, two bath, two-car garage. Single story. About thirteen hundred square feet. Easy peasy."

Paxton almost laughed. The way his sister-in-law

described the task at hand, she made building a house sound like playing with Legos.

He glanced at Quinn. "Did you know about this?"

Quinn frowned. "Can't say that I did."

Valerie shook her head. "The franchise has bought a lot near downtown."

"Where?" Paxton asked.

"I forget the street. The one where a house caught fire and burned to the ground. The house was a health and safety hazard. The city razed the actual house, left the foundation, and the charity bought it for a song. Owen promised to fit it in, so it's a go. The network loves the idea of charity work, and with the popularity of Construction Cousins, Tuckers Bluff is now on the map."

"Great. Next, we'll have folks from out of state rushing here and pricing the locals out of the market." Quinn blew out a sigh at his own words. "Present company excepted."

"Understood." She shook her head. "I really thought Owen would have filled everyone in on the details. Anyhow, the reason I grabbed you two is that Owen said you guys would be point on this."

"Us?"

She nodded. "That's what he said. Rules are the same for this as with all other of the charity projects. The family will be hands on as much as time permits. They have to do their sweat equity."

"Do they have to have any skills?" Paxton wasn't keen on having someone on a job site without experience working with power tools. That's how people wound up in the ER.

"No clue, but most folks about to receive the gift of affordable housing are eager to learn."

"Marvy," Quinn grumbled under his breath.

Paxton resisted the urge to agree. The network executives were the bane of his and his brother's existence. "I'm heading into town."

"Now?" Quinn's eyes widened.

"Owen is helping Jamison out at O'Faredeigh's. I think a little chat might be in order."

"Works for me." Quinn nodded.

His brother had to have lost his mind to have squeezed building an entire home from the ground up into their busy off season schedule. Though he did love the idea of a worthy cause, he didn't see how this was going to work. "What was my beloved twin thinking?"

"Oh, look! A playground." Sandra Lynn's son turned those puppy dog eyes on her. "Can't we stop and play? Just for a little bit?"

The last thing she needed was another stop. After driving for so long, all she wanted was to get to her mother's house, unpack what few belongings she'd managed to bring, and relish in the familiarity of her old room. At the least, she did not want to be driving anymore.

David had grown restless with the long ride. She couldn't blame him, five-year-olds and road trips across three states, including one as big as Texas, were never a good mix. For the last forty miles, he'd been dancing on her last nerve. She loved her boy more than her own life, but she wasn't going to take a long road trip with him ever again. Well, maybe once he turned thirty-five.

"Pleeeeease," David blinked at his mother.

Okay, maybe one more quick break would do them both good. She pulled into an open parking space. With most kids in school, they pretty much had the park to themselves. She'd barely come to a stop and David was out the back door and across the grass like a shot. Straight for the monkey bars. The really tall monkey bars.

Closing her eyes, she said a small prayer that her rambunctious son didn't wind up in the ER with a broken arm. Opening her eyes, she looked around at the playground that hadn't been here when she left Tucker Bluffs years ago.

So much had changed since she'd run off to marry Ed, but a few things were still as she left them. The café hadn't changed a bit, though her mom had told her that Abbie the owner had married a Farraday—one of the many cousins she had run around town and the ranch with during the summers when they were kids. And, of course, Sisters boutique. So many towns had lost their Main Street shopping to big-box stores. It made her smile to see that Tuckers Bluff still had a thriving business district. The familiarity pushed away the tension that had become a way of life for her. And there was the Cut n' Curl. Polly had been kind enough to hire her part time as a shampoo girl. It wasn't much, but any work would be a blessing. She would have much preferred her homecoming had been a triumphant return rather than slinking home, divorced, with her tail between her legs, but she was home. That was the important thing. She'd finally broken free from Ed Morton.

"Look, Mom, no hands."

She glanced up and forced a smile. Did Tuckers Bluff even have an ER? "Be careful. I'm going to call and let Grandma know that we're close." Pulling out her phone, she pulled up her mother's number.

"Sandra. Hey. I thought you'd be here by now."

"We made a few more stops than I'd planned, but that's a road trip with a restless boy. We're at a nice small park in town. We won't stay too long. I think we should be home within the hour. I figure it's best to let David run off some of the built-up energy."

"Good idea. That's what he probably needs. He's been cramped in your car for hours, and in that tiny apartment for too long."

Her husband—ex-husband—had insisted on a fancy modern apartment as if they were young swinging singles and not a family with a boy who needed fresh air and space. At least now he would have it. "Thanks, Mom."

"Love you, baby, and get him good and tired out." Her mom chuckled. "He's all boy."

Why her mother thought she knew anything about raising boys, Sandra had no idea. She'd been an only child herself. Something she hadn't wanted for her son, but now, it looked like history was doomed to repeat itself. Not that she'd been raised by a single mother. Her dad had been the best. Made her feel like his princess her whole life. It was one of the hardest parts of moving away with Ed. Her dad had begrudgingly thrown them a wedding, but made it clear to Ed that he didn't approve of him. At the first possible excuse, Ed had dragged her away to Chicago and wouldn't even let her come home for her father's funeral. She really should have listened to her father. But, of course, she wouldn't have David if she had. Glancing over at her son now swinging so high that she wondered if the swing set's metal legs wouldn't pull right out of the ground, she smiled. *Boys.*

Glancing over at Sisters, a list of things she was going to need ran through her head. Thinking on it, she'd drop David off at her mother's for some grandmother loving and run to Sister's. Her gaze drifted back to David. Oh, how she loved that boy. "Daddy, I'm sorry you aren't going to get to see your grandson grow up," she whispered. She was sorry about a lot of things.

CHAPTER TWO

With David safely at her mother's, probably eating too many cookies and drinking too much chocolate milk, Sandra was free to shop. Parking in front of Sisters, she wasn't at all surprised it was still there. The two sisters, one tall, one short, one blonde, one a redhead—at least they were when she'd left town—Sissy and Sister were such a part of the town landscape, things simply wouldn't be the same without them.

A bell above the door jingled when Sandra pushed it open. The scent of the place brought back memories of shopping with her mom for school clothes, birthday gifts, Christmas gifts, and pretty much everything under the sun short of what they'd buy at the hardware store. So little had changed, those were probably the same clothing racks from her childhood.

"Welcome to Sisters. I'm Sissy. What can I get you?"

Sissy hadn't changed. She was still tall and slender, and a redhead.

"You look familiar." Sissy cocked her head. "I don't forget a face."

Could she really remember Sandra? Or was this a sales ploy? Of course the woman should remember her, a few years and a few pounds hadn't changed her that much. When had she become so jaded? Oh, right. She'd run away to marry Prince Charming and wound up with Mr. Hyde. She's divorced and jaded. "I grew up in Tuckers Bluff. Left when I got married."

"Sandra Lynn, is that you?" Sister, her blonde beehive hairdo as big as ever, came out from behind the dressing room curtains. "I'd know that face anywhere."

Sissy's eyes lit up. "That's right. Your mother was in earlier this week. So excited to have you and her grandson under her roof again she was bubbling like an overflowing glass of champagne."

"What can I get for you today?" the other sibling asked with a broad smile.

Oh, how she'd missed all the smiling faces. In big cities, people stomped past, slammed doors in your face, and looked at you crazy if you smiled. It took Sandra a long time to remember not to smile at strangers. With the mention of each item on her list, the two sisters bustled around gathering what she wanted, occasionally raising a couple of items out for her to choose. There wasn't any better customer service than in this place.

Wrapping up her purchases, Sissy glanced up. "You thinking of staying a while?"

"For the foreseeable future." When she'd escaped the confines of this small town, she'd thought she'd never look back. Now, she couldn't wait to settle in and make a life for herself and her son. A good life. A small part of her still hoped for the fairy tale.

"How lovely." Sister's smile widened. "I know your mama missed you."

Sandra already knew that. Her mother had been coaxing her to come home ever since David had been born, and twice as hard since her dad died. Once she'd finally found the nerve to walk away from a bad marriage getting worse, there was no reason to say no. "I'm here now."

"She is going to have so much fun spoiling that grandchild."

Sandra bit back a grimace. "Yes, I know."

"You have a great day." Sissy handed her the bag with all of her purchases. "And tell your mama how happy we are to have you and that boy of yours back home where you belong."

Where she belonged. Once upon a time she couldn't wait to get away from the confines of a small town and see the world. She sure hoped coming home wasn't a bigger mistake than leaving, but as hard as it was to admit, she didn't have a choice. "Thank you." Sandra tucked the bag into the back seat of her car and climbed into the driver's seat. She took a moment to soak in the warmth of her interaction with the sisters. Yes, everyone knew your business, but she needed to remind herself that it was only because they all cared. She shuddered at the challenges of the busy place where she'd raised her son. Coming home might be difficult, but staying would have been worse. Here her son could breathe and enjoy his childhood. And living with her mom would give her the time she needed to get on her feet and save some money. In her mom's big backyard, maybe they could build the tree house David always talked about. Not that she knew how to build one, but that's what YouTube videos were for.

Enough lollygagging, she put the key in the ignition, but instead of the loud hum she'd expected, there was not a sound. "No. No." She turned the key again. "You can't die here."

The last thing she could afford at this stage of the game was car repairs. She tried again, as if the first two tries didn't count. Her heart pounding, she rested her head on the steering wheel. "Really, car? You only needed to go a few more miles."

A deep voice carried into her car through the open window. "Is there a problem, miss?"

Miss. Sandra looked up into the greenest eyes she'd ever seen. No, she'd seen those eyes before. A very, very long time ago. Back when she believed in dreams and princes and happily ever afters.

Paxton knew a damsel in distress when he saw one. He also couldn't resist helping one. That's how he was now looking under the hood of a car that should have died miles ago. Low on water, oil, and who knew what else, the car had to be running on love because it sure wasn't running on anything else. "New in town?" Paxton made idle chit-chat as he poked at a few wires.

"Sort of. We've been driving for days. You'd think it could have lasted a few more. Do you know what's wrong with it?"

Paxton knew his way around an engine as well as any guy, but he didn't see an easy fix. "Might be the starter. You'll have to call Ned. If anyone can get this old girl running again, it's him. I can give him a call if you'd like. Unless you have someone else you can call to help?"

She shook her head.

"Give me a minute."

"Is Ned very expensive?" Her expression told him this was not her first encounter with hard times.

How was he supposed to answer that one? "Depends. Starters could cost anywhere between five hundred and a thousand dollars."

For a moment she looked about to cry. "I should sell it. I can walk anywhere in town for the most part." Nodding at the car, she muttered, "Have to sell."

"Of course, it could be something else." Watching her struggle to maintain her composure unexpectedly twisted his gut and he found himself needing to somehow make things better for this stranger. "Maybe it will be a cheap fix."

Again she bobbed her head, nibbling on her lower lip. The gesture seemed oddly familiar.

His call disconnected, and Ned from the garage on his way shortly, Paxton tipped his hat at her. "I'm Paxton, by the way. I'd be pleased to wait with you and take you home if you need a ride."

"Hello. I'm Sandra." An unexpected grin touched the corners of her mouth for a short moment. "And no offense, but I hope Ned can bring Betsy back to life with the turn of a screwdriver or maybe a kick of the tires."

Skipping over the kick the tires comment, his mind stopped at Betsy. She named her car. How cute was that. Between the introduction and worrying about getting the car running, the woman flashed another brief smile. He couldn't help but feel there was something familiar about her, but if she was new in town then he couldn't possibly have met her.

"I think this car has as many miles on it as it can, but Ned over at the garage can work miracles."

Facing the car, she mumbled to herself, just loud enough for him to hear, "A miracle would be nice" then she pulled out her phone and frowned.

"What's wrong?"

"It's dead."

Paxton removed his from his back pocket. "If you have someone to call, you can use mine."

She shook her head. "That's okay."

As Ned promised, he pulled up with his tow truck—just in case. Five minutes later he was shaking his head and hooked up her car. Paxton couldn't hear their conversation, but from the way she wrung her fingers together and nibbled on that lower lip, he knew whatever Ned had to say, she didn't like it.

As Ned climbed into the tow truck, Sandra walked up to him. "If the offer of a ride is still open…"

"My pleasure." He held the door while Sandra climbed into his truck. She gave him an address just at the end of town. When he pulled into the driveway, he scanned the old Victorian. "They don't make houses like this anymore."

"It's my mother's."

A little boy came running down the front steps. "Mommy, Mommy, look what Grandma gave me!" Filled with glee, the little boy waved a paper airplane as though it were a private jet.

"How nice." His mother leaned over to admire the small toy. "Go tell Grandma I'm here."

Gathering her packages out of the back of his truck, Paxton felt an unexpected pang of disappointment. Where there was a son, there was a father, and that made this sweet enigma off limits.

"Sandra Lynn," a voice called out from inside the house.

Sandra Lynn? His memory was firing on all pistons.

"There you are." A woman whose face seemed almost

as familiar as Sandra's came hurrying out of the house. "Sandra Lynn, you do know how to make a mother worry."

Holy, moly. No wonder the faces all seemed familiar. "Sandra Lynn Baker?" he muttered softly.

"Yes." For the first time since he found her slumped over her steering wheel, a sincere smile bloomed. "I didn't think you recognized me."

"Sorry it took so long."

"I'm the one who should apologize. I had you at a disadvantage. You still have the same face. I, on the other hand, look really different without long hair and braces."

Yes, the braces were gone, her figure had obviously filled out, and her shoulder length hair that framed her face was at least a foot shorter than the single pony tail that had hung along her back, but those steel blue eyes, high cheek bones, and sweet smile was still the same.

She stuck out her hand. "Nice to see you again, and thanks for the help. I really appreciate it."

"Which Farraday are you?" Smiling, the older woman squinted at him.

"Mom, this is Paxton. He brought me home. My car died in front of Sisters. He was nice enough to save me."

Slapping her hands together, the woman's grin widened. "Well, thank you, Paxton Farraday. I've got cookies just coming out of the oven. Won't you come in?"

Paxton touched his hat. "Sorry, ma'am. I've got some business to take care of, but maybe a rain check?"

"Any time."

"I'd better get inside too. See what David is up to." Sandra stuck her hand out at him. "Thanks again."

Bobbing his head at her, he wished he didn't have to go find Owen. "My pleasure. If you need anything else, let me know." Just because she was married didn't mean he couldn't help an old friend in need. He whipped out a business card and handed it to her.

Her gaze lingered on the card before sad eyes lifted to meet his. "Thank you."

Turning away and hurrying back to his truck, he wondered what the story was with Sandra Lynn and those sad eyes. And why did he wish more than anything else right now that he could do something to put that smile back on her face.

CHAPTER THREE

"**M**y, that Paxton Farraday sure did grow up nicely." Sandra's mom pulled the cookie sheet out of the oven.

Sandra also thought the man had filled out quite nicely. Those eyes were the same, but now they seemed to hold wisdom and some humor. What had those eyes seen since they were kids? When she'd recognized him, she'd been tempted to ask why had his family stopped coming to visit all those years ago. The first couple of summers without the Oklahoma Farradays had felt off. Nothing seemed right without him and his brothers. Yes, she still played with Grace and went gigging frogs in the creek with the other Farraday boys, but she'd missed laughing and joking with her friend. Eventually, like everything else in the world, life moved on and change became the new normal.

Setting the shopping bags on the table, Sandra unpacked her purchases while David ran around, flying his new plane in the backyard. She was going to have to get used to letting him have more freedom to roam, but for now, she could keep an eye on him through the large window above the sink.

Her mother puttered around the kitchen. "He's a good boy. You know he's on television."

"Television?" Her gaze darted to David outside. "What are you talking about?"

"Paxton. He has a TV show."

Paxton was an actor? Though the image didn't fit, how had her mother not mentioned that before? Or maybe she had, and Sandra had let it go in one ear and out the other. Sometimes her mother rambled on about people Sandra had never met, or who had moved to town after she'd left. Then again, she would have been interested in what Paxton was up to. All the Farradays were nice. Her childhood had been a blast playing with the massive family. She'd always wished she could have come from a large family. Had hoped to someday have a large one of her own. So much for dreams. But of all the Farraday boys, Paxton was the one she'd connected with, the one who always made her smile. They'd been playing together since she was David's age. When the older boys were off tipping cows or some other silly thing, they'd be fishing in the creek. It had taken her a while not to find the worms icky, but she'd loved the quiet of the fishing hole more than Grace or Hannah so she'd become Paxton's fishing buddy. She'd really missed their time together when they'd stop visiting from Oklahoma.

"He's on a show called *Construction Cousins* with most of his brothers. I've seen every episode. The show is really popular. They're renovating the old ghost town, Sadieville. Remember it?"

Somewhere in the back of her mind she seemed to remember her dad taking her by some old buildings that looked like a TV western, but she couldn't swear where it was.

"Anyhow, they're building housing out there as well, and it's helping put Tuckers Bluff on the map." The pride in her mother's voice was unmistakable.

Sandra nodded. "I'm going to clean up here, then bring our bags and things up to my room. I figure we'll put David in the bedroom next to mine."

Her mother averted her eyes and made a muttering noise, "Well, about that."

Sandra turned to look at her. "About what?"

"About your room."

This wasn't the first time she'd seen that expression on her mother's face. Whenever her mom looked like that, Sandra knew her mom was about to say something she would not like.

"Well, your room isn't available right now."

"Oh." It was silly of her to think her mom would have

preserved her room as it was. "I guess David and I can share the other room."

"Well." Her mom's gaze dropped. "I sort of had to rent them both out."

Sandra blinked. "What?"

Her mom wiped her hands on her apron. "I had to."

Someone else was sleeping in her room? A stranger? "Why? I thought you and dad were set after selling the ranch house and moving into a more affordable home in town."

Her mother frowned and leaned against the counter behind her. "Yes and no. Yes, it's more affordable, but we didn't get as much for the ranch as we may have led you to believe. This house has a hefty mortgage and without Dad's income, and the only thing I've ever known how to do is keep house. I just couldn't keep up. New roofs aren't cheap and we need one, then there's the ordinary expenses and repairs. It costs a lot to heat and cool this big old house."

"Oh, Mom." Her mother had never mentioned her financial troubles. Even though she never really had much while married to Ed, she still would have tried to help, but now her finances were tighter than ever and her first paycheck wasn't going to be much help. "Why didn't you say something to me?"

"I didn't see the point in worrying you at first, then when you decided to divorce Ed and talked of coming home for a while, I was afraid if I said anything you might not come back."

"Mom. I'm sorry. You should have said something."

Her mother waved a hand. "It's all fine. I'm handling it."

"Still, maybe I could have done something."

"You had your own troubles."

Talk about an understatement. If she hadn't been too proud to face it, she would have known from the start that marrying Ed had been a mistake. At least now she was home under her mom's roof again. They could work this out. "Where are David and I sleeping?"

"I've already put a rollaway for David in my room. You

and I will share the king bed."

"Well, looks like we'll be roomies." Things could be a lot worse. At least she had a family she loved, a roof over her head, and, tapping the card in her pocket, a new old friend. Maybe.

Paxton was beyond frustrated with his brother. Owen had finished up with Jamison and returned early to the ranch. The drive into town to track his brother down had been a waste of time. Except for bumping into Sandra Lynn, but right now, he was mostly annoyed at Owen's leaving the rest of the family out of the loop. "You do remember how to use a cell phone?"

"I know, but Mom was blowing up my phone. You know how much she wants us home in Oklahoma. She thinks if she wears me down that I'll wear the rest of you down. I'm sorry, it slipped my mind."

Quinn squinted at their brother. The man didn't say a word, but his eyes said a whole lot.

"Slipped your mind?" Paxton glared at his twin.

"Now, now." Aunt Eileen waved a spatula at the three nephews wandering around the kitchen helping set up for supper. "Everyone's allowed to make a little mistake here and there."

"Little? It's not like he forgot to pick up eggs at the grocery store." Paxton sighed. His aunt had a point, sort of. It was unlike his brother to spring something this big on them without warning. Owen knew better than anyone how backed up they were with projects off camera and on since the show had made them more popular than ever. "At least if we'd gotten an email about it I would have been better prepared when Valerie brought it up."

Quinn shook his head. "You're no better at reading emails than memos no matter who sends them."

Paxton shrugged. "Maybe not, but it would have been something to stop us from looking like idiots."

"No one thinks any of you are idiots." Aunt Eileen shook her head and smiled at them. "Handsome yes, idiots no."

"Is he still upset about the new house project?" Morgan came into the kitchen and kissed his aunt on the cheek.

"You heard?" Paxton shifted his attention from Owen to his other brother.

"The whole family knows by now." Morgan's wife came in behind her husband. "Next time I'll make sure to follow up with everyone when we do major changes to scheduling."

She smiled so sweetly at Paxton before glancing adoringly at her husband. It was impossible for Paxton to stay angry with anyone who made his brother so happy.

"City council is thrilled as well," Valerie explained. "Most of the time these houses go to single parents or injured vets. It's all for a really good cause."

His sister-in-law didn't have to drive that home. He got it. His family had driven home that philosophy since childhood, to those who much is given much is expected. Heck, even when things were tight with the ranch back home failing, they still made time to give of their time and talents if nothing else.

Aunt Eileen shooed everyone into the dining room, handing each person a dish to carry. "Did you hear that Sandra Lynn Baker is back in town?"

"As a matter of fact," Paxton held out the chair for his aunt to sit, "I gave her a ride home earlier today."

"Really?" His aunt looked up at him with curiosity in her eyes.

"She was downtown. Her car wouldn't start. Had to call Ned to help. I didn't make the connection at first."

"Her mother lives in that massive Victorian at the edge of town." Uncle Sean volunteered.

"Yes. That's where I dropped her off. I was surprised. She used to live out this way."

His aunt nodded. "They sold it and moved to town when Sandra Lynn started high school. Something about easier for her to be in town than isolated out here. But I always thought there was something more to it. When her dad died and Alice started taking in boarders, I was a bit sad to find out my suspicions had been spot on."

"So," Quinn scooped out his favorite mashed potatoes and handed the plate to his right, "what have you gotten us into?"

Morgan and Owen proceeded to explain about the lot near the edge of town and how they were going to build on the old pier and beam foundation making things easier and less expensive, but most of what his brothers said was rolling past him. His mind was stuck on Sandra Lynn, her broken-down car, her sad eyes, and wondering where was her husband?

CHAPTER FOUR

"At least we have an intact foundation." Neil pointed to the rear of the structure. "This part of the house didn't suffer as much as the front where the kitchen was, so we'll be able to salvage some of the exterior walls. That will save time. Now." Neil, the architect in the family, spread his initial drawings on the makeshift plywood work table.

Paxton looked around at the site of the mostly burned to the ground house. At least one positive he could think of at the moment for his work was that tilling under the mounds of ash surrounding the former home would be good organic fertilizer for the miserable clay crud that passed for soil in Texas.

"Pier and beam makes redesign much easier, not to mention that will save us money, too," Owen glanced around.

Paxton looked at the drawings then the existing foundation. "Same footprint as this foundation? How many square feet?"

Neil looked up at him. "Still thirteen hundred, but much more efficient. As you can see, I've added a rear entry garage. The original house didn't have one. Families don't want to unload groceries and children in the heat or rain."

Paxton could agree with that. "Good thing there's a big yard even with the driveway and garage added on." Looking at his brother's plans, he could picture what the place could be. Already ideas for plants once the house was built were swimming in his mind.

A car pulled into the driveway.

"Grace promised to bring lunch," Owen said without

looking up. "This way we won't lose any time. There's a lot to do and a crazy tight schedule."

"The more the merrier." Paxton chuckled. "Think she's any good with a hammer?"

"She's a lawyer." Neil frowned.

"Hey, I'm a landscaper but I know how to use a drill and milk a cow. What's your point?"

Shaking his head, Neil rolled his eyes and pointed to the salvaged walls. "Everything that couldn't be saved is gone. All of this is remaining. Structurally the walls are fine."

The sound of laughter and giggles filled the air as not one but two women climbed out of the car. Paxton stood a little straighter, recognizing both of them.

"Hey, guys. Look who I found coming out of the Cut n' Curl as I was leaving the cafe. Remember Sandra Lynn?" Grace waved one of the bags she carried in Sandra's direction.

Owen nodded. "Sandra, nice to see you."

"Isn't it great to have her back?" Grace looked happier than a kid at Christmas.

"You back for good?" Quinn asked with a smile and Paxton had to fight an absurd urge to tell his brother to back off.

Sandra smiled at everyone. "I am back for good. We moved in with my mother. For now."

A sweet smile made it to her eyes, and Paxton couldn't stop staring. First woman in ages to capture his attention for no good reason and she had to be married.

Grace hooked an arm around Sandra's. "It's been too long. It'll be wonderful having my old friend back again. We have so much to catch up on."

Neil turned to his brothers. "You have any questions?"

All the brothers shook their heads. After all, they knew how to read blueprints and there was nothing outstanding about any of the things on the drawings.

"Then I'm off." Neil turned on his heel, and glanced at Sandra. "Welcome back."

Owen spun about. "Let me catch a ride with you back to my truck. I've got some supplies I need to pick up."

Grace glanced at her watch, her eyes widening. "Crud. I didn't realize the time. I wish I could stick around, but I have a client appointment in ten minutes. I'm sorry I won't be able to drop you back at your mom's."

"No problem, I can walk from here."

Grace hurried away but turned at the last minute. "Hey, I have a great idea. Why don't you come out to the ranch for dinner? We can really catch up. Aunt Eileen is dying to see you too."

"I'd love to, but maybe another time. My car is still at the shop and Mom insists she doesn't need a car living here in town."

"No problem." Grace looked to Paxton and Quinn standing side by side. "One of you guys can bring her out. Right?"

"Sure," Paxton agreed a little too quickly, once again silently reminding himself that Sandra was a married woman.

"Bring David," Grace added as she slid into the car. "There will be plenty of kids to play with. You can come any time."

Sandra waved at Grace and then looked up at Paxton. "What time do you want me to come back to ride to the ranch?"

He shrugged. "We're about to get started on some of the framing. But with only half a day, it won't be a long day."

Her gaze darted to the pages on the wooden table and then up at the open space.

"Would you like to see what we're going to do?"

She nodded. "Yes, that would be lovely."

The first thought to pop into his head was that nothing could be as lovely as she was. His second thought was, back off Paxton. Too bad he liked his first thought better.

When she'd gone into the Cut n' Curl for her morning shift today, the last thing Sandra had expected was for fate to have left her alone with Paxton. She couldn't resist smiling. As much as she wanted no part of a new relationship, at least there was no harm in admiring the scenery. Paxton was tall and broad and as attractive as Texan boys can be.

Glancing around, she wondered what this project was all about. "I thought Mom said y'all were renovating Sadieville."

"This is for a charity. Not part of our TV show." He almost put his hand on her lower back to move her along, and instead settled for waving an arm towards the still standing walls.

"Do you often build houses for charity?"

"This is our first project with this charity. Sometimes back home, we did things to help out seniors or troubled families, but nothing to this scale."

"This is a great location. Not far from Main Street, but setback enough up the street to have a neighborhood feel. I love the tree-lined street. Not an easy find in West Texas."

Quinn began working on the framing as they moved across the empty space.

"Y'all are going to do this just the three of you?"

"All of us will be on it, and for a build of this size, and the speed, we'll bring in some of our crew, but the way this charity works is that the future homeowner has to put in sweat equity by helping around the build."

"Skin in the game," she said.

"Exactly." He waved his arm. "Now we're standing in the future kitchen. There will be patio doors leading to the backyard. Over here," he took a step around, "is the breakfast area."

"So many homes have opted for an island with stool seating and eliminated kitchen tables. We need it for homework and projects that don't mess with mom cooking in the kitchen."

"Yes." He nodded. "That's why Neil always finds a way to fit it in."

As Paxton kept talking, Sandra took in what a perfect house this was going to be. Not too big, not too small, practical, well situated, and the coveted big backyard she'd dreamed of for David since the day he was born.

"Outside is my domain." His words broke her thoughts.

"You take care of landscaping?"

"Yes, but I will help inside as needed. We all know how to do more than our primary jobs. Neil is the architect, but he wields a hammer and drill with the rest of us."

"And this is for who?"

"All we've been told is a needy family. I know sometimes they're veterans, sometimes it's a single parent, but no matter who, it's going to be worthy."

Paxton led her to where Neil had said the garage would be.

"Oh, wow. An attached garage is not common around here." She loved the idea. The more common breezeways in this part of the country weren't bad, but an attached garage is just so much better when juggling groceries and babies. Not that she would be having any more babies, but still.

"How much do the families have to help?"

"We don't expect them to be contractors."

Sandra nodded. "What do you expect them to do?"

"Clean-up is more helpful than you think. Then just about anyone can use a hammer. But most people can be taught to handle small power tools."

She looked up at him to see if he was joking. "Power tools?"

"Drills are easiest, if they're comfortable, a circular saw to cut two-by-fours." At that moment, the buzz of the saw sounded as Quinn measured and cut a few boards.

"I can't imagine." Give her nails to polish or someone's hairy eyebrows to wax and she's a pro. On a construction site, she would be useless.

"It's not hard. Just takes practice."

Done with the cutting, Quinn shifted to drilling in screws and Sandra shook her head. "I have my doubts."

Paxton chuckled. "Wait here."

Not sure what he had in mind, she walked a few steps back into the kitchen. Or what would be the kitchen? She could see it all so clearly. What a perfect home for someone.

"I promise this isn't hard. Let me show you how to use a drill to put in a screw." Paxton appeared with a piece of wood and a drill in hand.

Her heart fluttered. She had to stop herself from lifting her hand to her chest. Surely this had nothing to do with working beside Paxton and everything to do with power tools being seriously out of her comfort zone. It had been a long time since she'd noticed butterflies in her stomach. Butterflies that seemed to get more rambunctious every time Paxton looked at her. Had to be a coincidence. It had to be the power tools. She wasn't ready for anything more than simple friendship. Besides, what were the odds of anyone as sweet as Paxton wanting a woman who came lock, stock, and barrel with plenty of baggage and someone else's son?

"This is battery operated. We don't use corded tools anymore because the cords wind up getting cut or causing a trip hazard." He pushed the trigger. "This makes it go. This switch here changes the direction of the spin."

"Change direction?"

"Yes, whether you're screwing in or unscrewing it."

She focused on the tool, surprised when Paxton chuckled.

"It's not a snake. It won't bite you."

If this were her ex-husband, she would have expected the thing to do just that. Ed never knew what the heck he was talking about.

"The screw goes on the tip which is magnetic." Paxton placed the screw on. "Let me do one and then I'll hand it over to you."

Watching the drill and board was easier on her nerves than watching the man.

"You don't want to push too hard or you can strip the screw. Take it nice and easy."

Nice and easy. Easier said than done.

"Your turn."

The drill was heavier than she'd thought it would be. When his fingers slid away, she almost dropped it.

Still smiling as if she weren't the biggest klutz on the planet, she inhaled as he wrapped his hands around hers.

"Here, let me help."

Willing her fingers not to shake, she put a screw on the tip of the drill and let the pressure from his fingers pull the trigger. The screw went straight in.

"See?" He smiled and pulled away.

Breathing more easily with him not standing so close, she also regretted his not standing so close. How crazy was that?

CHAPTER FIVE

"There will be other kids?" Overflowing with excitement, Sandra's son danced around her as she stood in the bathroom, applying the last coat of mascara.

She didn't normally wear much makeup, but her eyes always looked so drawn out and bland if she didn't at least put on a dash of mascara and a bit of blush. "I expect you to be on your best behavior and listen to what the adults tell you to do."

"Can we go?" Anyone would think the kid was on his way to the North Pole to meet Santa in person.

"We're getting picked up in five minutes. Go put your shoes on."

He bounced out of the room. His excitement would be contagious if she wasn't already just as excited about stepping back in time, even for one night, and even if it was with a young son in tow. Dinners at the Farraday's were always a good time. Great food and a family that actually liked each other. This would be a good experience for David. He needed to see what happily married people and large loving families looked like. Up until now, his only example of marriage and family had been her and his father's strained, almost embattled relationship.

Putting away her makeup, she took in her appearance. Not bad for a prodigal daughter.

"Mom, a truck just pulled into the driveway." David bolted out of the room and down the stairs.

Of course a Farraday would not only be on time, but respectably early. Her heart did its own little dance. She put a hand on her chest, and hoped like so much else in this old town, that little had changed at the Farradays.

When Sandra walked down the steps, she spied Paxton squatting, talking to David. Had her ex ever brought himself down to his son's level? Not once could she remember Ed relating to David as if their son really mattered. The sight made her heart do a two-step that had nothing to do with warm memories of sprawling ranches and big families. Now she wondered if Paxton had children of his own. The thought had her battling disappointment. And why? Paxton's personal life was none of her business. Besides, even if he were single, a good-looking and nice man like him had to have women throwing themselves at him. Attractive women without baggage.

David turned to her. "Mr. Farraday says they have horses where we're going."

"They do," she nodded. "And if it's okay with the Farradays, yes you can go see them."

"Yay!" The boy shot up in the air like he wore springs for shoes.

"But," she waved a finger at him, "remember you have to do what the adults tell you."

Struggling to stand still, David looked up. "Yes, Mommy."

"Okay, then. Everyone ready?" Paxton straightened to his full height.

"David, go get your jacket. It might be cold when we come home." Home? How had she not thought of that sooner? "Oh, dear."

"What?" Paxton's eyes filled with alarm as his head shot around in search of David.

"It just struck me. I don't know how we're going to get home after supper."

"Oh that." Paxton's shoulders eased. "Grace and Chase live here in town. I'm sure she's planning to bring you home."

That made her feel better. For a split second, she was ready to cancel the whole outing if it meant putting one of the Farradays out to bring her and her son all the way to town after dark. "Of course."

His gaze on David across the kitchen, searching for his jacket in the mudroom, Paxton smiled. "He's a sweet kid."

She took in a deep breath. "Thanks. I want him to grow up to be a sweet man—strong, but sweet."

"Is that why you came home?" Paxton turned to face her.

"The city is not where I want my son to grow up. Besides, every kid deserves to be close enough to his grandmother to be a little spoiled. Though, under the same roof may be a little too much togetherness, but it's best for now."

He nodded, then his gaze drifted upstairs and back to her. "Just you two coming to dinner?"

It took her a moment to realize that Paxton must not know about her sorry ex-husband. Odd, she'd have thought that news would have spread across the grapevine like wildfire on kindling. "Just us. Mom already has plans."

David bounced back into the foyer. "Now can we go see the horses?"

Rolling her eyes at her son's enthusiasm, she grinned and nodded. "Let's go."

David jumped even higher on the way out the door. Her gaze settled on Paxton holding the door for her then to her son skipping down the walkway. For the first time in a long time, it suddenly felt like being hopeful about the future wasn't just pie in the sky dreams.

As soon as Paxton opened the door, Aunt Eileen rushed up to them and completely ignoring him, scooped Sandra into a familiar bear hug. He couldn't blame her. He wouldn't mind giving her a big old bear hug himself. Which was probably why he needed to keep a safe distance. He wasn't sure what the story was with David's father, but until he knew more, he needed to keep his hands in his pockets and his thoughts to himself.

"So good to see you, Sandra Lynn. Welcome back to

Tucker's Bluff." Aunt Eileen's smile took over her face as she leaned over. "And this must be David. I think there are some kids in the backyard waiting to meet you."

David looked at his mother, who nodded and mouthed, *Be good.*

"I'll take him outside." His cousin Connor's wife appeared behind their aunt. "I can check on what that brood is doing." Pausing a moment, she called over her shoulder, "By the way, I'm Catherine, nice to meet you."

"Nice to meet you too," Sandra laughed as David practically dragged the woman toward the back door.

The appearance of her son in the kitchen created a flow of family members descending on Sandra from every corner of the house. She was greeted with smiles and hugs and one person after the other shouting out "remember when" until he and a few others were almost doubled over with laughter. Paxton had almost forgotten how much fun his summers in Tuckers Bluff had been with his family, especially fishing with Sandra Lynn. She was one of the only girls who wasn't squeamish with worms. Actually, she was the one who turned him onto old horror movies. They could watch Vincent Price movies till sunup if his aunt and uncle had let them.

Linking elbows with her childhood friend, Grace tugged Sandra into the cozy family room. "We need to catch up."

While the women lingered in the living room chatting, Paxton found himself in the kitchen with his brothers and cousins helping set the table and carry condiments and just about anything their aunt wanted into the dining room. After all, the Farraday household was modern before it was popular. With six sons and only one daughter, Aunt Eileen and Uncle Sean made sure there was no such thing as women's work or men's work. Everyone pitched in where needed, and that included setting tables and tossing salads.

Valerie came through the back door. "Sorry, had to take a business call."

"At this hour?" Paxton looked up at the kitchen clock.

"I got a call from the charity." Valerie snatched a cucumber slice from the salad. "Seems there's been a bit of a glitch."

Owen looked up from the basket of rolls he was about to carry to the dining room. "Glitch for us or for them?"

"Both." Valerie sighed.

Aunt Eileen looked up from the open oven. "Uh-oh."

"Well," Valerie shrugged, "it isn't too big an uh-oh. You guys have a lot of framing to do before it's safe for the intended family to come help, but the designated family is no longer interested in the house."

Now Morgan turned to face his wife. "Why not?"

"Apparently, they're having second thoughts about moving so far away from Abilene. They'd rather wait for another house to come through for them closer to a big city and family."

"Put this on the table." Aunt Eileen handed off the large meatloaf pan to Connor. "I don't see why we have to bring in strangers from across the state. You're not going to tell me there aren't plenty of needy people right here in our own county."

"I always thought it made more sense to have someone local," Owen said. "Small-town living isn't for everyone and there's a lot of time and money going into this only to have someone move in and hate country life."

Glancing at the women chatting in the living room, Aunt Eileen nodded. "Y'all do know that Sandra Lynn is going through a divorce. I hear that moving in with her mother is all she can afford. So far she's only working part time at the Cut n' Curl. Cost of housing is going up, even in Tuckers Bluff."

Several heads turned toward the other room and back before shaking it at their aunt. That would certainly explain why Paxton had yet to meet David's father. Or why no one had even mentioned him.

"Table's all ready." Connor came into the kitchen. "I'll gather up the kids."

"Great." Aunt Eileen smiled. "Dinner's served," she announced from the hallway. "Better not let the food get cold."

Chairs scraped and footsteps clacked against the hardwood floors as the group made their way to the dining room. Heads still together, laughing the way they used to as kids, Grace and Sandra Lynn took their time crossing the living room.

"I need to make sure David washes his hands." Sandra extricated herself from Grace's arm.

"Connor's one step ahead of you," Aunt Eileen said. "Everyone, take a seat."

A passel of kids, led by Connor, scurried into the room, heading straight for the children's table beside the main dining room table. Paxton watched as Sandra hovered over her son, helping him settle in with the other children, reminding him to mind his table manners. Not that Paxton would expect much from kids that age, but the little boy nodded at his mother and promised not to forget.

He could see the struggle in her eyes as she forced herself to back away from the table and join the adults. It must be tough for her to have to uproot herself again and move home. A glimpse of sadness in her expression pricked at his heart. There had to be something more he could do to help them feel truly at home.

Paxton managed to secure the seat across from him for Sandra. It was as close as he could get with Grace sticking to her like glue.

"So now what happens?" Owen asked.

Valerie shrugged. "I guess they start all over. There's a long list of people in need, the problem is not having someone else backing out again because we're out in the middle of small-town West Texas."

Handing a bowl of potatoes to Grace beside her, Sandra looked up. "What's happening?"

"The people assigned to the new house have backed out." Aunt Eileen reached for her glass. "Apparently, they don't want to leave the city."

Sandra shook her head. "They don't know what they're missing."

"Right." Grace grinned at Sandra.

"Seriously." Sandra reached for the salad. "This is a great town and that's going to be an amazing house."

"You can see that already?" Paxton turned his gaze to her.

"Of course. The plans are clear and I could see it all coming together as you explained what would go where. And that big backyard is fabulous for raising a family and maybe a dog or two."

Paxton turned back to Owen, whose gaze had narrowed and the muscle in his jaw twitched which meant his mind was working. No doubt the two men were thinking the same thing. But first, he would have to find out more about Sandra Lynn's situation. Maybe this would be a way to bring that smile to her face and keep it there.

CHAPTER SIX

S o far so good. Sandra Lynn pushed the broom around the empty stylist's chair. There was enough hair on the floor to make not one but several wigs. Not that they were saving the hair, but still.

"Here you go." Mrs. Brady smiled at her and shoved a bill into Sandra's hand. "It's nice to have you back."

"Thank you." She waved at the woman and waited until no one was looking to peek at the tip. The bills tucked in her palm made her smile. It wasn't much, but it was a start. She'd shampooed four different women's hair this morning and Mrs. Brady was the biggest tipper yet. At this rate, it would take a long while before she could afford to rent a place of their own for her and David, but she could be patient when she had to.

"Morning, Emily." Polly smiled at the woman coming through the front door. "I'll be ready for you in just a bit. Have a seat at the shampoo station and Sandra Lynn will get you ready."

The squeal Emily let out could have been heard clear to Oklahoma City. "I heard you were back! Why didn't you let anyone know you were coming home?"

Any lingering embarrassment that she felt from slinking home after a failed attempt at Prince Charming and happily ever after slid away at Emily Taub's excited greeting. "It all came together rather quickly. There was no time." Truth was, she saw her chance to get out of Dodge and took it. Her ex had spent the better part of the last two years drunk more than sober. When he refused to agree to regular drug testing, the judge had denied joint custody and given her permission to return to her hometown. If Ed wanted to see

David, he would have to make the eight-hour drive. Not the end of the world.

"Has Grace told you about our Friday Girls' Night?" Emily sank into the seat and leaned her head back in the basin as Sandra turned on the water and squirted her hands with shampoo. "Nothing special. Just us girls, maybe a movie or dinner. Sometimes we'll go over to the Boot 'N' Scoots in Butler Springs. With everyone so busy with kids and things we try to do Girls' Night at least once a month."

Giving her friend a brief massage, Sandra found herself smiling. Really smiling. It just struck her how nice it's going to be to have friends again. "Sounds like fun."

"Oh, good." Emily grinned. "I think our first night together should be a pajama party."

Sandra rinsed the shampoo out and wrapped a towel around Emily's head. "Do y'all do pajama parties?"

"Not usually." Emily sat up. "But once in a while to celebrate, yeah. And they're so much fun. And your returning home is definitely worth celebrating." Before Sandra could say a word, Emily threw her arms around her and squeezed. "Welcome home."

How had she been so blind to let Ed talk her into leaving everything she loved so dearly? "Just let me know which Friday and I'll make sure Mom can take care of David for me."

"Oh, that's right!" Emily sprang back. "You're a mom now."

Her cheeks tugged hard at the corners of her mouth. "My pride and joy."

The bell over the door rang and Mary Sue Carter, the afternoon shampoo girl, came into the salon. "Hey, Polly, Sandra. Sorry I'm a few minutes late."

"No, problem." Sandra glanced at the clock over the wall. Fifteen minutes wasn't going to make or break anything. "If you'll excuse me, I'm going to hang up my apron and get ready to head home. My son is probably wondering where I am."

Emily frowned. "He's not in school?"

"Not yet." Sandra shook her head. "I had to straighten

up some paperwork, but he should be starting on Monday."

"Your turn, Emily. Have a seat." Polly waved her customer over to her chair.

A few more rounds of *glad you're back* and *see you soon* floated back and forth before Sandra was able to grab her purse and head home. Thank heaven's Tuckers Bluff was small enough that if you had time, a person could walk anywhere. It was only about twenty minutes to her mom's house. A nice walk in good weather. And today, the walk flew by as her mind ran over all the wonderful blessings falling into place, one by one, since returning home. Soon, she'd save enough money to rent a little house for her and David and she could start giving him the life she'd always wanted for him.

At the curb of her mom's place, she was surprised to see a big truck. Wasn't that Paxton's? Making her way up the front steps to the porch, she came inside and expecting the loud sounds of a rambunctious little boy, she was surprised by the library-like silence. "Anyone home?"

"Hey, sweetie." Her mother called from the laundry room. "Washing sheets. David and Paxton are in the yard."

David *and* Paxton. In the yard? Crossing the kitchen to the back door, she drew to a stop at the sight in front of her. It took a moment, and then she realized her son was holding a hammer. What the heck? Another minute of silent observation and she could hear Paxton.

"That's right. Let the weight of the hammer bang on the nail. Want to try it again?"

Her heart tripped and her mouth fell open. Was Paxton actually teaching her son how to use a hammer? His voice was so smooth and gentle urging David on. Another swing, and from the way David spun around and smiled at Paxton, the sheer joy in his expression, she was willing to guess that her son hit the nail. Swallowing hard, she blinked back tears. She should never have left Tuckers Bluff.

Hanging out with kids was not the norm for Paxton, but this kid was just a bundle of energy and excitement that could make anyone smile, no matter how hard their day. "That's perfect. Now you've got the hang of it. Remember be careful with your thumb. I don't want your mother mad it me for letting you work with my tools."

David bobbed his head, and nibbling on his lower lip, held the nail and let the hammer swing down on it. Of course, even with momentum, a young boy like David needed to repeat the move multiple times, but what mattered is he did it on his own and he knew it. Until now, Paxton hadn't really given any thought to having a family, but these few minutes gave him a view of how sweet having a son of his own could be.

"Hello there." Sandra came walking out of the house toward them. The sunlight shined from behind her like a halo. Dang she had been a cute kid, but now, she was one heck of a beautiful woman.

"Hi." He turned to David. "That'll be it for today's lesson. I need to talk to your mom for a bit."

David frowned and Paxton wished he could keep at it a little longer, then the boy handed him the hammer. "Are you going to come back?"

"I said I would."

"And you're really going to help me build my fort?"

Paxton flashed a smile, hoping it would help ease the concerned frown on the little boy's face. "Absolutely."

"Really?" His frown was still in place.

A sudden pang of distaste pinched in his chest. What had this young child learned from adults that he didn't believe Paxton. "Really." With his pointer finger, he drew an x across his chest. "Cross my heart or hope to die."

That brought a huge grin to the boy's face. "Mommy." David spun around and ran up to his mom. "Paxton is going to help me build a fort."

"Is he?" She glanced over her son's head at Paxton.

"He promised." David's smile was infectious.

"Then I guess he's going to help you build a fort." Again, she looked over her son's head and leveled her gaze with his.

Paxton had no idea what was running through her head, but he quickly concluded that mom needed as much reassurance as her son had. With an easy smile, he nodded at her and just the way he'd done for David, drew an x over his heart.

"I smelled something delicious when I came home. Why don't you go see what Grandma has baking?"

"Sweet." Throwing a fist in the air, David did a little boy jig and sprinted into the house, the screen door slamming shut behind him.

"No pun intended," Paxton chuckled, stepping closer to Sandra.

"Not sure what happened here, but thank you."

"Honestly," he shrugged a shoulder, "I'm not sure what happened either, but I came by to talk to you about something, and David peppered me with questions about what I did and did I use tools and do I know how to use a hammer and does my mommy let me use a saw."

Sandra lifted her hand to her mouth and bit back a laugh. "I'm so sorry."

"Don't be." He shoved his hands in his pockets. They were safer there. "I grabbed my tool belt and showed him a thing or two. It was fun."

"He's told me before that he wants a tree fort when we get a house. I didn't realize he hadn't let go of the idea."

"Building club houses, and forts, and tree houses in our backyard is how my brothers and I got started in construction. We had a great time. Even if the first few efforts fell apart too easily."

Sandra's eyes widened. "I didn't know that. None of you fell out of a tree, did you?"

"No bones were broken in our learning experience."

"I can't help but worry about falling from a tree house. I wish we could build a ground-level fort instead."

"We can build whatever you want." Which reminded him why he was actually here. "Speaking of build, you mentioned you liked the house that we're building for charity."

She sat on the back stoop. "Who wouldn't? The place is going to be perfect."

"I don't mean to get personal. Your mom told me you're only working part time at the Cut n' Curl?"

"That's right. I was a manicurist in Chicago, but it's taking longer than I wanted to get my license in Texas."

Just what he and his brothers had thought. From what he'd seen Sandra Lynn fretting about paying for a minor car repair and what his aunt had shared over dinner, he suspected she and David could probably fit the charity's criteria. "We all had a chat after you left about the problems with bringing outsiders into a small town. First thing this morning, we had a long meeting with the network and then the charity. We insisted one condition to the network funding this project is that we have a local family move in. Both the network and the charity loved the idea of a single mom."

Her head tipped to one side as he spoke, but her face showed no sign of understanding what he was saying.

"There's some paperwork that would need to be filled out and filed, but that's mostly a technicality as our recommendation was accepted."

"Recommendation?"

He blew out a low sigh and said a fast prayer that she'd be as happy about this as he was. "We'd like the house to be for you and David."

"I'm sorry. What?" She did that cute head tilt thing again.

He was beginning to worry she wasn't going to like the idea of charity. "The network, the charity, and we Farradays all think the house should be yours."

Her eyes widened and before he could brace himself, she sprang up from the stoop, threw her arms around him and screeched in his ear. It took her a few moments of squeezing him before she backed up. "Sorry. I just can't believe it. You're my hero!"

If it meant another hug like that one, he might see about getting her two houses.

CHAPTER SEVEN

S andra stared at the piles of sawdust on the floor and all the scraps of wood, strewn packaging, and loose nails and other debris left behind by the workers. Never would she have pictured one crew could make such a mess. But her job was to clean up after the brothers, not critique their work habits.

Bottom line, they were building her and David a house. Every time she thought about it, she did a little jig at the idea that she would be a homeowner. She'd never lived on her own. She'd gone from her parents' house to living with Ed, and then back to her parents'. Until a few days ago, she never dreamed she'd have a home of her own. *Take that, Ed Morton.* Liquored up, when she'd finally found the nerve and saved enough money to leave, he'd slurred from the sofa that she'd come crawling back.

She shrugged off the thoughts of him and swept away the mess. But it was a mess in her house. Not anyone else's.

"Coming through," a deep voice said behind her.

She scooted to one side.

"Other way," the voice called out.

She scooted in the opposite direction as a man hauled a stack of boards past her. "Sorry, I was in the way."

"No worries, ma'am." Boards piled on his shoulder, he paused and smiled at her. Even though a lot of the crew were from out of town, everyone on the build was really friendly.

"I'm Jet. You must be the homeowner." The guy stood in the middle of what would one day be her breakfast nook.

"I am." Just saying that sent a chill down her spine. "Or at least I will be. Nice to meet you. I'm Sandra."

He stared at her for a moment. Not long enough to be a problem, but long enough to make her feel uncomfortable.

"That must be heavy." She gestured to the load on his shoulder.

"This?" He gave the boards a look as if he'd forgotten it was there. "Just part of the job." Tossing a smile her way, he shifted around and trooped to the other end of the house.

Taking the giant metal dustpan and broom in hand, she began sweeping up the debris, still incapable of getting over that Paxton and his brothers had pulled some strings to get her this house.

Milling over all the fun things she hoped to do, how she would decorate David's room, where she'd place the sofa—once she bought one, of course. That had her frowning, staring at the opposite wall. She wasn't homeless, but her situation had not been ideal. She'd had to leave all her belongings and secondhand furniture behind with her ex. She debated if it was too soon to start hitting garage sales in search of the perfect furnishings. Though that might be rushing things a bit.

"Need some help?" Jet unexpectedly appeared behind her.

Turning quickly, more from surprise than anything else, his eyes darted up to her face, and she knew she'd caught him staring at her butt. No point in making a fuss about it. "Nope. I've got this. It's part of my sweat equity."

His gaze dropped momentarily before leveling with her eyes again. "Call me if you change your mind and want a man's help."

"Will do." In some other lifetime. She hadn't been a part of the dating scene for a heck of a lot of years, but she still recognized a man's interest when she saw it. But too bad for Jet, she most definitely was not interested. Spinning around to return to her task at hand, she somehow got her foot tangled between the broom and some plastic wrap on the floor and dropping the broom, her arms flared and she wobbled in place. Strong hands manacled her arms.

"Whoa." Jet held on, steadying her.

"Oops." She found her balance, but Jet's hand lingered

on her arm. Glancing down at the fingers that still held on to her, she took a step in retreat. "Thanks, but I'm okay now."

"You sure?" He still held on.

"I promise I'll watch where I put my feet."

He released his grip, but remained too close for comfort. "I'd hate to see you get hurt."

If he wasn't going to back off, she certainly was. Her hard hat had wobbled and she placed back on her head properly. "I'm sure I'll learn how to navigate a construction site."

Jet nodded. She couldn't swear to it, but she thought she saw disappointment in his gaze. "Just be careful."

"I will."

Leaning over to pick up the broom she'd dropped, a string of cuss words came from the front of the house. Straightening quickly, she looked through what would be her front door to the front porch. Paxton stood, muttering, frowning, and holding his hand. "Uh, oh."

Paxton had seen Jet lingering around Sandra and then holding on to her arm long after he should have let go. Paxton was glad that Jet had been close enough to stop her from falling over, but that didn't mean he had to like it. And he didn't, not one bit. Jet was a player. He had a string of women from here to Oklahoma. That guy was the last thing Sandra needed.

Distracted keeping an eye on Jet and Sandra Lynn, he'd lost his grip on the old board he was stripping and sliced his hand open on a protruding nail. The sting of his hand was almost as sharp as the sting of watching Sandra manhandled by Jet. Putting pressure on the wound, he debated going in search of the first aid kit, or laying down some house rules for the crew where the new homeowner was concerned.

"Are you okay?" Sandra appeared at his side.

"Yeah. Just a little nick."

"Nick? Let me look at it." Her gaze fell on the blood

oozing between his fingers. "You're bleeding. Is there a first aid kit on site?"

"In the construction trailer." They'd set up a trailer in the far corner of the backyard.

"Keep the pressure on it. I'll get the kit and be right back."

Had this been a competitive sprint, she'd have won the gold medal. In half the time he would have expected, she'd returned with the first aid kit and a small bucket of fresh water as well as a roll of paper towels under her arm.

"Thanks. I can take it from here." As much as he wanted to feel her touch, he didn't dare let her.

"Nonsense. Give me your hand."

As soon as she poured cool water on it, he winced. Maybe it was a bit deeper than he'd thought.

"You need to be more careful, Paxton."

"Tell me something I don't know." He'd been an idiot for letting Jet's attention to Sandra get to him. "Listen, I'm sorry for the swearing earlier."

She waved away his comment. "Nothing I haven't heard before."

Why did that raise his hackles?

"Relax." She used the paper towels to wipe the wound. "Are you up to date on Tetanus?"

"Always." That was one thing that he and his brothers insisted on for all the crew. Rusty nails and sharp objects abounded on construction sites.

"That's good to hear." She continued to clean the wound and then fished through the kit.

"Not exactly how I'd hoped your first day with us would go." He tried not to wince when she squirted something on the cut.

She shook her head. "It's not that bad."

"I said that."

"Not the cut." Looking up at him through long lush lashes, she chuckled softly. "The antibiotic ointment."

When she pressed a non-stick gauze pad onto his palm, he reflexively pulled away.

"Come on now. David doesn't wiggle this much."

"Sorry." He smiled at her. "I'll try and do better."

That pulled the desired smile from her. Taking hold of the roll of tape, she unwound a long strip and wrapped it around the sterile pad. "The bleeding has slowed, but you may want to see Brooks. You might need stitches."

"I'm sure I'll be fine. You're doing a good job at doctoring."

She studied his freshly wrapped wound. "This will have to do for now. But you'll want to hold it up against you for a bit until it stops bleeding completely."

"No time. I have work to do." He should get back to work, but her holding his hand had been the best part of this day. Her hands were soft and efficient. A part of him considered that nothing seemed more important to him right now than keeping this gentle connection. Short of slicing his other hand open, he wouldn't mind finding a reason every day to hold Sandra's hand. So not a good idea. A recently divorced woman, with a young son, finding her way back home. She didn't need the complications of an infatuated Farraday.

"Lying down on the job?" Quinn came up the front walkway.

"He cut himself." Sandra Lynn snapped the lid of the first aid kit shut.

Quinn frowned. "How bad?"

"Just a nick," Paxton repeated.

Sandra's brows rose high on her forehead. "Not a nick. I still say you should go see Brooks."

One of the downsides of having a cousin who was a doctor was there was no excuse for not going to seek medical advice. Relatives always fit you in.

"You need the rest of the day off?" Quinn asked. "Ryan's bringing another load of plywood. We can handle it without you."

"Nonsense. I'm fine." To prove his point, he turned his hand, palm out, delighted to find no sign of blood on the fresh bandage. "See? I can work." At least he hoped he could. If this had been his right hand, he'd have been screwed.

"Hmm," Quinn huffed. "Up to you." Clearly satisfied, his brother proceeded into the house that already had all the exterior walls up and the guys in the backyard working on framing out the roof.

Pushing to his feet, he turned to Sandra. "Break time over, but with only one usable hand for now, I'll shift to working with Ryan inside. At least I can manage a drill without any trouble."

Shaking her head, Sandra made a tsking sound. "You know, you're more stubborn than my son."

"Since I like David, I'm going to take that as a compliment."

Another smile bloomed on her face. Oh, boy, was he going to love keeping her in smiles.

CHAPTER EIGHT

"I appreciate you shuttling me back and forth to the job site," Sandra said.

The commute allowed her more time to spend with Paxton. Even if it was a short commute and she wasn't pursuing him, she still enjoyed his company.

"Same time tomorrow?"

"I need to work at the Cut n' Curl in the morning. I can walk over."

He glanced her way as he pulled into the driveway of the charming Victorian. "I don't mind picking you up from work. I know a person can walk everywhere in Tuckers Bluff, but why walk when I can give you a ride?"

She didn't want to inconvenience him. "You sure?"

"I'm more than sure." He gave her that lopsided Farraday grin.

The front door opened and her mother rushed out. That was odd. Something had to be wrong. Sandra didn't wait for Paxton to open her car door. She was out of the vehicle like a shot. "Mom, what's wrong?"

"What's wrong?" Her mother repeated the question stopping in her tracks.

"Why are you practically running out of the house? What's wrong?"

"Nothing's wrong." Her mom actually rolled her eyes. "I wanted to talk to Paxton."

He was already out of his truck and circling the front of his truck to where they stood. That same smile adorned his face. "What can I do for you?"

"I was hoping you might stay for dinner? I got a little carried away in the kitchen and made enough food for my boarders and a small army. Since I don't have a lot of freezer space, I'll settle for a man with a healthy appetite."

Paxton looked from one woman to the other. "That's mighty thoughtful of you."

"Mom." Sandra turned to face Paxton. "I know you've had a long day. If it's not convenient, I'm sure my mother will take a rain check." She didn't know about him but after a hard days work, she would kill for a long hot shower. Especially if she was going to be sitting across from Paxton at the dinner table.

"What better after a long day than a good home-cooked meal." Her mother's eyes suddenly sprang open wide. "Not that your Aunt Eileen isn't a good cook. She certainly knows her way around a kitchen, but it is a long drive back to the ranch." As her mom often did, she spoke first and her brain engaged later and now was trying very hard to backpedal. "What do you say?"

She flashed her mother a cross-eyed look, but her mother just smiled back.

"I'd love to stay for dinner. That would be great." He followed the two women up the porch steps and paused by the doormat, stomping his feet, and brushing a days work off his boots. "I'm afraid I'm a bit dusty."

"No worries." Her mom waved him inside. "We all track in this Texas dust anyway."

Sandra had no idea how this happened, but thanks to her mom, Paxton was staying for dinner.

"Did you ask him?" David stood just inside the foyer, his contained nervous energy obvious to anyone with eyes.

"I did." Her mother winked at her grandson.

"Then he's staying?"

There was little doubt in Sandra's mind that her mother was not so subtly trying her hand at matchmaking, but it was also clear that her son very much wanted to spend time with Paxton.

"Yes, he's staying." Her mother spun around and pausing just long enough to gently run her hand down David's cheek in a tender gesture, she marched back to the kitchen.

David whooped and Sandra turned to Paxton. "I think you have a fan."

A chuckle rumbled out of him as he motioned for her to lead the way. "I hope he's not my only fan."

His words almost had her tripping over her own feet. What did he mean by that? Was he referring to her, or someone else? And why did it even matter.

From the kitchen, her mother called out, "David, why don't you go play outside until supper is ready?"

There was no need to ask her son twice. As she'd suspected was true of all little boys, he loved being outside and discovering all sorts of mischief. A moment later, the screen door slammed shut behind David.

Shaking her head at the noise, she turned to Paxton, ready to give him one last out. "If you have somewhere else to be, I'm sure my mother will understand."

"Nope. Nowhere else to be. I was planning on popping into O'Faredeigh's for dinner anyhow. But, if you don't mind, I'd love to at least wash my hands before supper."

"Oh, of course." She extended her arm to the opposite end of the foyer. "Powder room is that way."

Having left his hat in the truck, he bobbed his head and disappeared through the doorway.

While she waited, her mind began turning. If he had nowhere to go, did that mean there was no woman in his life? Could it be someone as handsome and nice as Paxton Farraday didn't have a girlfriend? Why did that thought make her heart leap? She didn't want anything to make her heart leap. She'd already had one man in her life. She did not need another. Not even Paxton Farraday.

The aroma of something awfully delicious smacked Paxton in the face as he stepped into the kitchen. "Oh, that really does smell wonderful."

"Hope you like meat loaf, mac and cheese, and fresh baked corn bread."

The woman really wasn't kidding when she said that she'd cooked enough for an army. "I love corn bread."

"Good." Alice Baker wiped her hands on her apron and reached for a stack of dishes.

"Here." He reached forward. "Let me?"

"Nonsense." She smacked the top of his hand. "Guests don't set the table. Go outside and enjoy a little fresh air. I'll call you when supper's ready."

He glanced over at Sandra, wondering if the right thing to do was to insist on helping, or doing as he was told. What he really wanted was to stay where Sandra was.

"You too." The feisty woman waved her hand in a shooing motion at her daughter. "I don't need a herd of people in my kitchen."

"Yes, ma'am." Sandra responded sweetly, but behind her mother, she rolled her eyes and gestured for him to follow her.

Outside, he saw David throw a football, but didn't make it very far. It had no spiral and Paxton wondered, had no one had ever taught David to throw? What was the deal with his father? Why wasn't he teaching his son how to use a hammer and throw a football?

"Toss it this way, sport."

David put all of his weight into the toss but it didn't wind up anywhere near Paxton.

Picking up the football, Paxton held it out to David. "Here, let's see if we can't put a little more oomph in that throw." Thankful he wasn't playing with a regulation-size pigskin, Paxton helped fold David's small fingers around the football. "If you put your fingers on the strings, and then hold it back by your ears before you throw it, the ball should spiral off of your fingers."

David nodded at the instructions, his gaze so intent it was as if Paxton had given him the nuclear codes. The boy held the ball with his fingers on the strings and cocked back his arm. This time the ball sailed further and there was a slight wobbly spiral.

"That's the way," Paxton encouraged him.

Meanwhile, Sandra stood behind them clapping. "Great job, David."

The little boy beamed at his mother and then shuffled his feet. "Do you know how to throw a baseball?"

Paxton had played all of the sports. He'd been partial to football. Played on the offensive line, subbing as quarterback for a game or two, but he liked baseball too. He patted the boy on the shoulder. "Sure do. Do you have mitts and a baseball?"

The boy lit up and raced off toward a plastic container set up against the house. He flung open the lid and pulled out the necessary items, then ran back and handed Paxton a mitt. "I hope it fits. My dad is shorter than you."

"It'll be fine, buddy." No point in explaining that height had little to do with mitt size. Sort of like feet. Tall or short didn't always play a part in shoe size.

Clearly more than a little excited, David ran to the other end of the yard.

"Let's start closer, David. I'd rather you work on technique than distance or speed, okay?"

Nodding with that same intense look on his face, David moved closer. "Here?"

"Right there, buddy."

David wound up and threw the ball. Better than with the football, but far enough away that Paxton had to reach out to catch it. "Not bad. Did someone teach you that?"

"Mom tried, but she throws like a girl."

He bit back a smile. "I bet she throws pretty good." Glancing over his shoulder at her still standing by the house watching, Sandra shrugged at him. He didn't know how she did now as an adult, but as a kid she'd kept up with the impromptu games at the ranch.

There were a lot of things he didn't know about the grown-up Sandra Lynn. Things he'd like to know, from her favorite color and food, to what really brought her back to Tuckers Bluff? Feeling foolish for simply staring at her, he waved at her, more delighted than he should have been when she grinned and waved back.

"Are we finished already?"

Turning back to the tossing session, David's head was cocked as he studied Paxton. For such an energetic young boy, he sure had some grown-up intensity. "Nope. Not finished. You ready to catch one?"

"Go ahead." David smiled.

Paxton casually tossed the ball. "What position do you want to play?"

"Shortstop." He scooped the ball up and threw the ball back as hard as he could. "Or catcher."

For now, he would be a little short for shortstop, but catcher would fit his size well.

"Did you play baseball?" David focused on the ball slicing through the air toward him.

"I covered first base. That's because I was the tallest kid on the team. You want that in case anyone overthrows. I could stop most things coming my way."

David nodded.

Paxton wasn't sure if the kid really understood, or was just being polite. Though what he really suspected was that this poor child was starved for male attention. The sad sensations that settled in his gut worked to remind Paxton just how blessed he'd been growing up. He had parents who paid attention, showing all their kids lots of affection and interest, and then he had all his brothers to play with. And for a while there, his cousins too.

Another ball came sailing towards him. Already David's arm was improving. "When can we work on the tree house?"

Knowing his mother wasn't thrilled about a tree house, he turned to see Sandra's reaction. Her smiling expression hadn't changed much in the last few minutes. The problem was he had no idea if she was smiling over her son's baseball skills, over helping David build a tree house, or if she was merely contemplating the immortality of the crab.

"Paxton?"

"Oh. Sorry, sport." Turning away from Sandra Lynn, he faced David. "How about I come over on Saturday and we work on it? We'll have more time then."

Almost bouncing in place, David nodded. "Sweet."

Taking a minute to glance back at Sandra, it struck him that he couldn't have said it better himself… Sweet.

CHAPTER NINE

"**D**inner is ready. Everyone wash up," Sandra's mother called from the kitchen.

Waiting by the door that David just bounced through, Sandra met Paxton's eyes. "You're good with him."

"Thanks." The comment caught him off guard. How hard was it to be nice to a young kid? "He's a really nice boy. I remember having that much energy when I was his age. Lots of days I wish I still had it."

"You and me both." She chuckled, the screen door slammed shut behind them as they entered the kitchen. "He is a bundle of energy. I have no idea how the teachers get him, or any of the boys, to focus in school."

"I'm not a parent, but having been a young boy once, I remember my mother throwing us all outside to burn off our energy. I suspect that's why schools have recess. So they burn off as much of that energy as possible outside the classroom."

"He wants to play baseball." Her gaze lingered out the window toward the large yard.

"That's good. He'll come home nice and tired."

"He still has to make the team." Her gaze darting back to his, she pressed her lips tightly together as she led the way into the dining room.

"Really? At this age I thought all kids get to play."

"You think?" The softness in her eyes returned. Not that he expected anything less, but it was heartwarming how much she cared for her son. Too bad he wasn't so sure about the boy's father. The question was on the tip of his tongue, to ask what was the deal with David's dad, but that was none of his business. He couldn't imagine having a son and not spending time with him. Even now, David's father was missing out on playing ball in the yard. Those were some of his best memories with his dad and brothers. "I could work with him to give him some more practice and help him play better."

A light twinkled in her eyes. "You would do that?"

Paxton shrugged. "Sure." Why wouldn't he? He liked the kid, and to his surprise, really liked playing with him, especially when the boy accomplished something new and grinned like an Olympic medal winner. But just as important, he'd be spending time with Sandra.

"But you're so busy."

"It's only time. Time is the greatest gift an adult can give a child."

Her face crumpled, and her voice dropped. "Too bad his father didn't think that way."

Paxton came within an inch of broaching the subject of David's father, instead, he snapped his fingers. "As a matter of fact, Quinn played varsity baseball. He was really good and I bet he'd be glad to help teach David the finer points of the game."

"Wait, you're telling me you're going to have your brother who never cracks a smile teach my son baseball?"

That had him laughing. "Don't let the grumpy face fool you. He's a marshmallow inside. As a matter of fact, I bet we can gather some of my nieces and nephews along with brothers and cousins and have makeshift games at the ranch. There's plenty of space for a baseball diamond."

She shook her head. "I can't let you drag your whole family into helping David learn to play."

"Why not?"

Her eyes rounded and her jaw dropped slightly open, slammed shut, then dropped open again, only no words came out.

"It will be fun for everyone. And who knows, maybe David will make friends with the next generation of Farradays. We all sure had fun together when we were kids." Grinning himself, he did his best to cajole a smile out of her. "Remember the time we had horse races across the field and not till you'd won on Shadow did Adam tell us that he didn't like having a rider on his back?"

"If I hadn't been so excited from winning, I might have passed out." She chuckled. "Shadow was a sweet horse."

"And only you could ride him." About to offer more thoughts on improving David's ball playing, her mother entered the dining room.

Standing in the doorway with David in tow, her mother beamed at them. Anyone could see the woman was delighted to have her family close by again. "We ready to eat?"

"Starved." Sandra's smile seemed to reach her eyes once again.

That made him happier than it should. He approached the back of her seat and pulled out her chair. The even brighter smile she tossed his way as she sat down made him so very glad his mother had taught him manners, despite his arguing that girls could pull out their own chairs as easily as boys.

Reaching for his hand to one side of her, and David's on the other, she bowed her head.

Her mother snagged Paxton's other hand to complete the circle. "Sandra, would you say grace tonight?"

Paxton listened to every heartfelt word. The Farradays still said grace before every meal—they had for as long as he could remember—but somehow, in such a small family setting, it felt different.

"Amen." Sandra lifted her gaze.

"Amen," the table echoed.

"Please pass the cornbread." David stuck out his arm. Apparently manners mattered to David's mother too.

"You can't eat just cornbread." Mrs. Baker passed the dish to her grandson.

The kid gave a momentary pout before nodding at his grandmother as she added a slab of meatloaf to his dish. "I also made your favorite. Mac and Cheese."

That totally changed the child's disposition and Paxton had to bite back a grin.

"Is that all you're serving yourself?" Mrs. Baker shook her head. "Don't be bashful at my table." Without asking, she took a large scoop of mac and cheese and plopped it on his dish.

Thankfully, he was hungry enough to eat it all, but his mama had raised him to always leave the table a little hungry when invited to a family's home for dinner.

David's eyes went wide. "You'll eat all that?"

"Hardworking men—and growing boys—need lots of good food." His grandmother smiled down at the young boy.

"Even the vegetables." Paxton stabbed at the broccoli and shoved it in his mouth, rubbing his tummy as if he'd just eaten a banana split. He had a feeling that Sandra would appreciate a little outside vegetable encouragement. "Someday you'll eat all this. Especially when you're on a growth spurt."

"I can't imagine what it must have been like cooking for all those Farraday boys," Sandra's mother added broccoli on David's plate.

Pausing his fork, midair, Paxton nodded. "The Farraday women can pack it away too."

Sandra's mother just laughed. "Oh, I bet those dinners were a sight to see."

Thinking back on family dinners, Paxton couldn't help but smile. "When we were all young and getting too rambunctious at dinner, my mother used to get frustrated and tell us we were more feral than the six younger brothers in Seven Brides for Seven Brothers. Of course, she was exaggerating." Instantly his mind flashed back to the time that Ryan threw a biscuit to Quinn and the next thing he knew, all six boys were tossing bread around like a baseball in a triple play. That was probably one thing Sandra would most definitely not want him to teach her son. Too bad, it was an awful lot of fun when he was five years old.

So much was going through Sandra's head as Paxton and David talked sports, dreams, and horses. Her mother laughed at way more than she should have but it was obvious to anyone watching that the woman was more than happy to have her only daughter and grandson home again. This is what family should have always been like. Why had she waited so long to make a change? Maybe because deep down she didn't want to admit her parents had been right and she had been a deluded young adult?

"Y'all go on into the other room. I'll clean up here."

Paxton pushed away from the table and standing up, lifted his empty plate and glass.

"None of that." Her mother shooed him away. "Guests don't clean up in this house."

"I don't mind."

All her mother did was put her fists on her hips and smile at him.

A moment later, Paxton set the dish back down on the table. "Yes, ma'am."

"Can I ride my bike?" David looked up at her.

That was one thing he'd not had in the city and Sandra was so very happy that her mother had given him one as soon as they'd arrived. "Sure, but you have to stay close enough for me to watch you from the front porch."

Pushing the porch swing so it moved slightly, Paxton watched David as intently as she did. "He'll sleep well tonight."

"That's the hope." Sandra lifted her feet letting the swing do its thing. She liked the slow back and forth rhythm as she watched David ride, turning in neighbor's driveways. She was hopeful that there would be children nearby for David to play with, but so far he was on his own. They fell into a comfortable silence, listening to David's commentary as he rode back up and down the driveway. She sucked in her breath when he lifted his arms and shouted, "Look, Mom, no hands!"

"David," was all she had to say for him to grab hold of the handlebars again.

Paxton chuckled. "They do say boys will be boys. We

all did. The worst that will happen is he'll fall over, scrape a knee or chin, then get back on and keep going. It's in our genes."

"I suppose I should be happy that living in the city he knows how to ride a bike at all." She'd made sure he could do that so he could keep up with the other kids, but with nowhere to ride in that dumb apartment, once he'd outgrown the old bike she'd bought at a garage sale, she hadn't bothered to replace it, until now.

The sun began to dip below the horizon. Sandra glanced at her phone, surprised at how quickly time had passed. A person could get used to this pace, and the company. Though she wasn't going there. Not now. "David. Five more minutes."

"More time. Please?"

She shook her head. "It's late. You have to take a bath and get ready for bed."

"Yes, ma'am." The way the poor kid sighed anyone would think she'd told him he'd have to eat another plate of broccoli.

"Like I said," Paxton shrugged at her, "boys will be boys. My mother would set a timer for us. It had bright colors. She'd place it on the porch rail and once it went off, we were done. We could negotiate with her, but not that timer."

"Never thought of that. Might be a good idea." She glanced at Paxton. He must have a thousand places he could be other than this porch swing. "I didn't mean to keep you here this late. You've got a long drive back to the ranch."

"The ranch and the road aren't going anywhere. This is…" he glanced from David to her, "nice."

Her heart did that little flutter thing that both excited and scared her. Shaking her head, she looked at her watch. "Time's up."

David pulled his bike up to the porch. "I'm tired."

She almost shouted hallelujah. Some nights, getting him to settle down when he'd spent all day indoors was challenging. Tonight she suspected he was going to collapse before they said their prayers.

The bike nestled into a corner on the porch, David shuffled his feet, hesitating.

"Let's get going," Sandra nudged him forward.

The kid's feet seemed to root into the wooden floor. "Mr. Farraday?"

"Yes?" Paxton stood beside her.

"Can you stay and read me a story?"

Before Sandra could say anything, Paxton spoke up. "I'd love to, sport."

David's face could have lit up the neighborhood. "Really?"

"Really."

For the first time in ages, there was no need to negotiate bath and bed time. David raced into the house. From where she stood, she could hear her son calling out. "Grandma, can I take a really fast bath?"

The words floated out onto the porch and Paxton actually chuckled. How could any one man have so much patience with a child that wasn't his?

She motioned for Paxton to follow her inside. "Why don't you have a seat for a minute. I suspect this will be the fastest bath in the history of bedtime."

"Don't rush on my account."

"Oh trust me, I won't have anything to do with it."

By the time she reached the top of the stairs, David was already wrapped in a towel. Turning to her mother, she didn't say a word, but the question was obvious.

Her mom shrugged. "He even managed to wash behind his ears. Clean as a whistle."

Another minute and David was in his pajamas and calling down the stairs for Paxton to come to their room.

By the time Paxton took the steps two at a time, David had already crawled into the folding bed. It was hard to miss the way Paxton casually glanced around the room, his gaze pausing at the bed, the two nightstands on either side covered with books, creams and what nots that two women kept at their bedside, then over to David. "All ready, buddy?"

David nodded and handed him a book. The story had

been one Sandra had loved as a child.

Seated at the foot of David's bed, Paxton opened the book to the bookmark. His voice took on a beautiful cadence as he turned each page doing every voice and every sound effect. Even Sandra could have fallen asleep to the melodic tones of the rise and fall of his words.

Her son snuggled further down into the covers, no doubt lulled deeper into his exhaustion by Paxton's delivery.

This man was the real deal. The kind of man that made a woman believe in knights in shining armor and Prince Charming. Somehow Paxton Farraday seemed to be both; just the thought of it warmed her to her toes. She needed to get a handle on her imagination, there simply was no way her upside down world could lead to happily ever after. Her gaze drifted back to Paxton, pulling the blanket up over the sleeping child's shoulders as he softly whispered, "Sleep tight, buddy." Then again, didn't they say that truth was stranger than fiction?

CHAPTER TEN

Giving Sandra a ride on an almost daily basis was out of character for Paxton. Having gotten to know her and her son, there was no doubt in his mind that choosing them for the house had been the right thing to do, but the more he got to know Sandra Lynn the adult, the more he appreciated any time alone with her, even if it was in the cab of his truck for the short ride to the construction site. The house was coming together faster than they'd expected. The original plan had been for the Farraday Construction company to do all the work, but for a worthy cause, just about every Farraday who could wield a hammer or work a skill saw had shown up for at least a few hours to give a hand. Never had they been so far ahead of schedule.

"Everything okay?" Sandra asked from the passenger side of his truck.

"Absolutely." He'd spent a great deal of time the last week just sitting back and watching the movement of the sun, determining what parts of the property were in shade or sun or some combination. Once he'd gotten a good feel for the available space and the lighting, he'd been able to put his ideas on paper.

"You've barely said a word since we left Mom's."

Paxton pulled up in front of the house. It really was coming together. This was going to be the perfect home for Sandra and her son.

Opening the passenger door, she climbed out of his truck, then turning to face him again, leaned in slightly. "Are you sure nothing's up?"

Paxton pulled the drawings for the landscaping out from behind the seat in his truck, and climbed out of the car.

Totally out of character for him, he'd been nervous about letting Sandra Lynn know his plans were done. He had worked hard on them, doing his best to keep the personalities of the new homeowners in mind, and he was proud of the results. More than anything, he really wanted Sandra to be happy. In just a few short weeks, she'd become very important to him. "I have something to show you."

"Okay." Her brows buckled and her voice almost cracked.

He smiled. "Relax, it won't bite. I promise. I have the landscape design here." He held them up.

Her eyes lit up and a smile took over her face. "Ooh. Can I see?"

"Of course." He pulled the papers out of a tube and laid them on the hood of his truck. "These are just a first draft. You get full veto power. Whatever you don't like, we can come up with something else."

"I don't know that I've ever had veto power before." She laughed. "I'm sure I'll love whatever ideas you've come up with."

He sure hoped so. Standing close enough that their arms touched, he sucked in a deep breath and dropped a leather weight on each side of the drawings to keep them from rolling up again.

"Wow." She looked from left to right of the massive paper. "I can't draw a stick figure. This is amazing."

So far so good. He blew out a breath that had been stuck in his throat while he waited for her initial reaction.

Squinting, she pointed to one side of the drawing. "So I gather all the pretty colors are flowers?"

He nodded.

"Walk me through it all, please."

"Of course." Most clients required explanations of his plans, but none had meant as much as this project. He wanted desperately to give Sandra and her son the perfect home. Not till this moment did he realize just how badly he wanted her to like what he'd done. "I've done my best to give you what I think you'd like while staying within the budget."

"Thank you." She smiled sweetly. "Not that I'm paying for the plants out of my pocket, but I know the charity's parameters are quite strict."

"I chose low-maintenance items since I know how busy you are with work and David, and you've mentioned a time or two that you have a brown thumb."

"You were listening?" She tipped her head to level her gaze with his.

"Always." He was more than listening, he'd taken in every word and catalogued them in the back of his mind. "Unless you have a particular love of gardening, then I could put more items that need attention. Just remember, if there's something special you'd like me to add, I can find a way to make it work."

She put a hand on his arm. "Paxton, I'm sure it's all perfect. If I develop an unexpected interest in gardening, I can always plant other things once the house is mine."

He looked down at her delicate fingers resting on his arm and swallowed, hard. "Okay." He flipped the page and pointed to the back corner of the property. "We'll start in back. Right here we'll plant both Golden Rod and Milkweed. This will attract a good number of butterflies. I thought David would enjoy that. Often I use Prickly Pears to attract butterflies, especially if the homeowner is a cook and interested in making Prickly Pear jam, but I didn't think it was a good idea with an energetic little boy running around."

"Oh, I like that. Butterflies are so pretty."

That had been what he wanted to hear, that he'd guessed correctly. "Most of these shrubs along the back are drought tolerant. There were lots of prettier options, but I figured that you'd prefer low maintenance."

"You figured right." She smiled, returning her attention to the papers in front of them. "What else?"

He explained about the six-foot wood fence, a staple in Texas home ownership, and a few other things before circling back to the empty spaces in the backyard. "There's room for anything that interests a young boy and his friends; a swing set or a trampoline—"

"Or fort," she interrupted.

"Yes." What he really wished is that the backyard had better trees to build a low tree house that would ease her concern and still make David happy. A good live oak would do the trick, but in this part of the country, large trees just weren't that common. "There's lots of space in the middle of the backyard for playing. Maybe I can talk David into a nice big fort? Especially now that he's in school and will be making friends."

"Friends." Lips pressed tightly, she nodded. "We didn't have many friends in Chicago."

He'd noticed that even after starting school, David hadn't seemed to make a lot of friends yet. Of course, even though Tuckers Bluff was a small town that was growing, lots of kids lived far out on ranches.

Looking up, Sandra's gaze darted from the drawing to each direction he pointed to in the front yard as he explained about the Nandinas with their pretty red foliage and the combinations of perennials, grass and stone.

When he finished, he rolled the papers up again and slid them back into the tube. "So, what do you think about all this?"

Sandra looked around at the yard and what Paxton had envisioned. There was only one thing missing. She looked up at him. "Do you think there's room for a peach tree?"

"If you want a peach tree, we'll fit in a peach tree." Paxton looked at the house then back to her. "Where would you want it?"

Instead of asking to see the plans again, she wandered around the corner to the backyard. Stopping nearly dead center of the yard, she spun around, her arms out, thinking about all the delicious fruit they'd have in a few years. "Right here, Paxton."

"Right there sounds good."

She stepped several feet to her left and spun again. "Am

I pushing my luck if we plant two?"

That had him chuckling softly. "I don't think two peach trees will break the bank."

Lunging forward, she almost hugged him, but instead stopped mid stride. The job site was no place for public displays of affection, even if it was nothing more than friendly gratitude. She couldn't believe how everything was coming together. She'd always wanted a house, fruit trees, a big yard, and who knows, maybe one day a dog. Little boys should have dogs. No matter how you sliced it, all of her dreams of home ownership were coming true.

"Would you like more?"

This time she couldn't resist. The man was just so dang amazing, squealing with joy, she practically jumped up and down before throwing her arms around his middle in a squishing bear hug. He was solid and warm and she had to fight not to melt into his shoulder.

In the awkward way men did when they didn't know what else to do, his hands patted her back. Stiffly at first, and then, when she didn't move, his arms settled around her. "Should I offer to plant four trees?"

Realizing how awkward it was to be hugging him in the middle of the yard, she reluctantly let go, and taking a step back, looked up at him. "I'm sorry. I guess I got a little carried away."

Like a laser, his gaze seemed to bore right through her. What she didn't have a clue about, was what he was thinking.

"No, worries." He shoved his hands in his pockets. "I've just never had anyone be this happy over a tree."

She laughed. "I guess it's silly, but you listened to me and actually planted a fruit tree." Maybe something so small shouldn't make her so happy, but it did. After all, she'd been through in the last few years, she would take her joy where she could find it. And in Paxton's arms seemed to be a very pleasant place to start.

"You two having fun yet?" Holding back a chuckle, Jamison came up the walkway.

Hoping she wasn't blushing all the way to her toes,

Sandra took a quick step back. "We're talking trees."

"Trees?" This time Jamison flashed a full-blown smile that seemed to shout that he didn't believe a word she'd just said.

"What are you doing here?" Paxton pulled his hands out of his pockets and crossed his arms.

"I've got a few hours free. Thought I'd give a hand. Unless, of course, you don't need it."

Paxton pushed away from the truck he'd been leaning against. "The more the merrier."

Jamison actually sputtered.

"Don't even think about it," Paxton scolded his cousin.

Holding his hands up in the air, Jamison shook his head. "I didn't say a word."

"No." Paxton moved forward his expression almost menacing. "But you were thinking about it."

Knowing where their minds had probably gone, the interaction between the two cousins was almost as fascinating as the plans for the landscaping of her new house. She'd always enjoyed being a part of the large Farraday clan, but at the moment, with his fists clenched at his side Paxton looked ready to slug his cousin. "Gentlemen," she interrupted.

Both heads whipped around to face her.

"Don't we have work to do?"

The two men nodded at her.

"I'll head on in the house and see where I'm needed." Jamison nodded at Sandra and darted up the front steps into the house.

"I guess it's my turn to apologize. Sometimes my cousins are more childish than their children."

"To quote a friend of mine, no worries."

As she'd hoped, that made him smile. But too soon the smile slipped and a serious tone took over his face seconds before he started to reach forward and then quickly, instead, shoved his hands back in his pockets. "Since tomorrow is Saturday, is there any chance I could talk you into joining me for dinner? As much of a pain as Jamison can be, he runs a fun pub."

All the air in her lungs rushed up and caught in her throat. Was this dinner as in a date, or as in friends?

"I'm sorry." He took a step back. "I shouldn't have—"

"No." She cut him off. "I mean yes. I'd like to join you for dinner tomorrow night."

A broad smile appeared and made his eyes sparkle. "Great. I'll pick you up after David's bedtime. Is that okay?"

"Perfect." The air had returned to her lungs and her cheeks hurt from smiling. She still didn't know if this was a date, and had no idea what she wanted, but one thing she did know, she really wanted to have dinner with Paxton, and she wouldn't mind another hug too.

CHAPTER ELEVEN

Paxton looked around at his siblings and cousins pushing away from the table, carrying empty plates and glasses into the kitchen. With a brood this size and growing, Aunt Eileen ran the household with more efficiency than the Marine Corps. Even though he'd never been in the military, his cousin Ethan constantly confirmed the Marines had nothing on his aunt.

Owen brushed up beside him, his wife Connie only a few steps behind.

"Bro, what's got you so quiet?" Owen asked.

"Not much." He glanced at his aunt standing by the sink and smiled. "Just thinking about the immortality of the crab."

"Oh, I've heard that one before." Chuckling, Connie walked past the two brothers.

The truth was that Paxton had been thinking about Sandra and that unexpected hug pretty much all day. He could not remember the last time he looked forward to a date as much as he was to their date tomorrow.

The dishes piled high on the counter, the clean-up crew gathered around the sink, loading the dishwasher, scrubbing pots, drying whatever was hand-washed, and doing general kitchen cleanup. The rest of the group had retreated to the back porch to watch the kids playing in the fields. He was going to have to arrange for that baseball game he'd mentioned to Sandra.

"You've got that look on your face again." Owen came to stand beside his brother at the railing.

Having Sandra on his mind so much had thrown Paxton. So many things were dancing around in his head.

"How did you know that Connie was the one?"

Owen blinked. "The one? One what?"

"You know."

"No. I don't." A buckle formed between Owen's brows. "Wait. You mean as in the only woman for me?"

Paxton couldn't bring himself to say yes, he merely kept his gaze on the horizon and shrugged.

His brother chuckled softly, then slapped his brother on the shoulder. "What did I miss?"

"Nothing. Just thinking." He wasn't ready to share everything with his brother yet.

"Thinking." Owen sighed and leaned over the railing, the toe of his boot resting on the bottom of the railing.

"There was something about her that drew me to her and I couldn't imagine living the rest of my life without her." Owen shrugged. "Even if she was annoying as all heck when it came to design ideas."

Connie walked onto the porch and up to her husband. "What has you two looking so serious?"

"Life, liberty, and the pursuit of happiness," Owen shot back without skipping a beat.

"Comedians." She rolled her eyes at her husband.

"Sorry, couldn't resist. Just telling my brother about how I fell head over boot heels in love from the moment I saw you."

"Aww," Connie cooed, leaned in for a quick kiss, and then chuckled. "Maybe it was the second moment."

As much as Paxton had been happy for all his brothers who had found their someone special, for the first time he actually envied their easy relationship.

Leaning back, Connie smiled at her husband. "The coffee is brewing. Do you want a cup?"

"Sure." Owen nodded, his gaze fixed on his wife, his eyes twinkling with sheer happiness.

Connie spun around. "Paxton, would you like a cup?"

"No thanks."

As Owen's wife made her way into the kitchen, Adam got up from the rocker a few feet away and stood at Paxton's other side. "Couldn't help overhearing. You thinking about settling down?"

"I didn't say that. Was just curious how you all knew that your spouse was the one?"

"Just curious, huh?" Adam chuckled. "When I first saw Meg, I thought she was an angel."

"That's right." Paxton snapped his fingers. "She was broken down on the side of the road in her wedding dress."

"And feisty as hell." That brought a smile to Adam's face. The same sappy smile all his brothers wore, and yet Adam had been married for a lot more years.

"That's when you knew?" Paxton really wanted to understand.

"Not that day, but she sure stuck in my mind. Like all the time, finally it struck me that I didn't want to live without her at my side. When I couldn't imagine going through the day to day without seeing Meg, I knew."

Paxton mulled that over. He certainly was spending more time than was reasonable thinking of Sandra, and even David. He did know one thing, he loved getting to see Sandra Lynn every day, and the thought of losing that when the build ended gave him an unpleasant kick in the gut.

Apparently, he must have a sign over his head flashing confused man, because Dale, his cousin Hannah's husband, joined in the conversation. "What's got everyone smiling like fools?"

Paxton tore his gaze away from the horizon and looked at his brother and cousin. The two men really were grinning like the fool on the hill. His mind kicked over to Sandra Lynn twirling in the yard over a peach tree, and the corners of his mouth tipped up in a hard smile.

"See? Now you're doing it." Dale settled along the rail beside Paxton. "What are we talking about?"

"Women," Adam answered at the same time that Owen muttered, "Wives."

"Ah." He looked to Paxton. "You thinking of getting hitched?"

Shaking his head vehemently, he waved his hand for emphasis. "No. Just… thinking."

"Mm." Dale stared off into the distance. "First time I

spotted Hannah, I spooked her horse with my motorcycle. Once I saw the fire in her eyes, there was no getting her out of my mind."

Again with the constantly on their mind thing. He resisted the urge to sigh. Paxton glanced over his shoulder as more of the couples were gathering on the porch. The family sure seemed to have an awful lot of happy couples. Then his gaze turned to the kids running around playing.

"Gotta get that energy out before bedtime." Connor joined the group. He'd married a woman with a young daughter. Not that anyone watching his family would know she wasn't his daughter. His cousin's words had him thinking of David playing in the backyard with endless amounts of energy.

"Well." Adam slapped Paxton on the back. "Just keep an eye out for a big gray dog and a woman, then you'll know."

Connor rolled his eyes. "I still remember when Gray knocked Grace over at Chase's feed store. By then we were all believers."

Paxton had heard the stories of the matchmaking dog, but by the time his brothers had moved here, Gray and his mate seemed to have settled down to ordinary ranch work. Then again, maybe a wise dog showing up to play matchmaker would make life easier. He chuckled softly to himself. Who was he kidding? He didn't need a matchmaking dog to know that as much as he'd liked Sandra Lynn as a kid, as a man, he was way past smitten and on his way to falling—hard.

A small part of Sandra missed when her son was an adorable toddler, splashing around in the bathtub, giggling wildly over bath bubbles or bobbing rubber duckies. Another part of her was thrilled that he was old enough to play in the tub without her hovering over him. Worn out from working the shampoo station this morning and the construction site this afternoon, today was a day when she was more grateful for David's growing independence. Tomorrow might be another story.

"You look awfully tired." Her mother rinsed a dish and stuck it in the drying rack. "Maybe this construction work is too much for you?"

The same thought had crossed her mind, mostly when she'd reach for something and her back complained, or last week when she accidentally hammered her thumb instead of the nail, but if she asked to cut back on time, then she wouldn't see as much of Paxton, and she really liked her time with Paxton. A whole lot. "No. It's not too much."

Throwing the dish towel over her shoulder, her mom turned off the running water. "Then if you're not tired, why do you look so serious?"

"Just thinking, I guess." She grabbed another rag and began drying the dishes.

Her mom spun back around and turned the water back on. "You know, everything will work out. It always does."

"I know."

Casting a sideways glance in Sandra's direction, her mom sighed. "Doesn't look that way. Tell me what it's all about?"

She shrugged. "I suppose I thought by now my life would be different. A husband, siblings for David, my own house."

"You are getting the house."

That much was true, and she was so excited watching it come together. Neil even incorporated some of her ideas into the design so now there was a small linen closet for towels in each bathroom as well as a hall linen closet big enough for pillows and blankets. "I am happy about that, but I feel like time is running away from me."

Her mother stopped rinsing and looked out the window at some unknown point. "I never thought I'd grow old without your father." She turned around. "And don't get me wrong, I miss him every day of the week, but I have a nice life now. It's different than what I'd thought, but it's a good life, and I'm happy."

Feeling awful for not having been here for her parents, she wished she could do so many things differently. Moving to stand closer to her mom, she wrapped her in a hug. "I love you."

"I love you, too." Her mom kissed her cheek and turned back to the sink. "You'd better go check on your son before he shrivels into a prune."

Bobbing her head, she gave her mom one more kiss on the cheek and turned on her heel toward the stairs.

"And one piece of advice," her mom called out to her. "Don't be afraid of change. You might be surprised at how happy you can be."

Even though her mom didn't come right out and mention Paxton, Sandra knew full well that was what the woman was referring to. Her parents had been high school sweethearts. If her father had said it once, he'd told her a hundred times that friendship was the strongest foundation for a happy life and marriage. She had to wonder if she and Ed had ever been friends or if she was simply so desperate to escape small-town life that she fell for the first guy who promised to whisk her away. Not that it mattered. Ed was her past, now she had to figure out her future.

David was still in the bathtub playing, happily unconcerned that his fingertips had shriveled like raisins. Deciding that a few more minutes of playtime wouldn't hurt anyone, she sat on the floor, just enjoying watching him play. When she next glanced at her watch, several minutes had passed. "Okay, David. Time to get out."

To her surprise, he didn't ask for more time, he climbed out and stepped into the towel she held for him. Once he'd dried off, put on his pajamas and climbed into bed, he handed her his favorite story to read. "Mom?"

"Yes."

"Do you like Paxton?"

"Of course I like Paxton."

"I like him too."

That actually made her smile. "He's a nice man."

"He plays catch with me, and I really like how he reads bedtime stories. Even more than when you read."

"Oh, really." She tickled his tummy, delighted when he giggled at her.

"If you really like him then he'll keep coming around."

"Whether or not I like him has little to do with what Paxton does. He's a busy man."

His smile slipping, David nodded. "I guess."

"But as long as we're building our new house, I'm sure we'll see plenty of Paxton."

"Can I go work on the house too? I know how to use a hammer. Paxton taught me."

"Oh, sweetie, construction sites aren't safe for children. Even I have to wear a hard hat. But I'm sure one day soon, when the crew isn't there, we can go look. How does that sound?"

"Is tomorrow too soon?"

That made her laugh. Kid's sense of time was pretty pitiful, but in this case, she couldn't blame her son for his curiosity. "Maybe not tomorrow, but I'll talk to Paxton and see what we can do."

"Thanks. He's nice, he'll say yes."

"Good night." Placing the sweetest of kisses on his cheek, she wondered how much longer she'd get away with that, and then she thought about what her son had said. Was it wrong of her to want Paxton to keep coming around as well?

CHAPTER TWELVE

"I like the red one." Sister bobbed her head at Sandra Lynn.

Sissy, on the other hand, shook her head. "Nope. The blue one. It shows her curves, but isn't in your face like that cleavage to her belly button red dress."

Cleavage to her belly button was probably an exaggeration, but it was much lower cut and she didn't want to give Paxton the wrong idea. On the other hand, she was totally smitten and wanted to put her best foot—or dress—forward. Frustrated with everything in her closet, she finally decided that savings was good, but a new dress for a date with Paxton was better.

Staring at the blue short-sleeve sheath dress with a square neckline that showed just a hint of cleavage, she decided that Sissy was probably right.

Strolling home from Sisters, the blue dress in the pretty pink bag, she realized that she had not missed having a car. Her car was so old, Ned was having a hard time finding one last part she needed, but walking down Main Street she considered if just selling it didn't make more sense. She'd have a little extra money to stash in her almost depleted emergency fund. That would make a lot more sense. Of course, it helped to have at least one vehicle in case of emergency. Though she couldn't imagine anything that would require driving, she was too aware that fate had a way of laughing at people when they pretend that all was well with the world.

Turning the corner on her mother's street, her gaze immediately darted to the old Victorian set back from the curb. As much as she'd hated giving up the ranch land, during high school she had loved living in town. Hopefully, her son would learn to love Tuckers Bluff, and unlike her, wouldn't be tempted to leave due to young adult wanderlust. Reaching her mom's house, she turned the knob and stepped into the old house. Expecting David to come barreling across the house to greet her, finding the house so quiet always surprised her. Setting the dress on the chair by the entry table, she started for the kitchen when her mother came trotting down the stairs and scurried right past her.

"Where's the fire?" she followed after her mother.

"David's not feeling well. I convinced him to lie down in bed. Now, I'm going to make him my special apple peel tea. See if that settles his stomach." Her mom was already pouring water into a pan.

Nodding, she took a step in retreat. "I'd better go check on him."

"Go on up. Maybe seeing his mama will make him feel better."

Halfway up the stairs, her mother let out a screech muffled with a very unladylike string of words. Unsure of who needed her more, she figured her mom had most likely left David nicely tucked into bed. On the other hand, she had no idea what was going on in the kitchen. "You okay?"

Eyes squinted almost closed, and her arms shoving towels into the sink, her mom appeared to be doing her best to stifle the eruption of Old Faithful. Water was shooting from every corner of the sink. "What the heck?"

"Turn off the water!" her mom shouted, the water now spraying her right in the face.

"Oh, my." She skidded to a halt at the site. "Out front?"

"No. Under the sink."

Under the sink? Of course. Scooting down, surrounded by growing puddles, she opened the lower cabinet doors and practically crawling under the sink on all fours, she turned the hot water off first, praying her mother wasn't being spewed with scalding water. The valve shut tight, she turned to the blue valve to the right and turned until the handle stopped and the sound of gushing water slowed. Backing out from under the sink, she had never been so relieved to no longer have running water, and so thankful that no one had seen her crawling around on all fours.

Pushing to her feet, her mother was already running to the linen closet. While Sandra grabbed a few dry dish rags from a drawer to sop up the water pooling on the floor, her mother ran in with a stack of bath towels.

"It's times like this I really miss having a man in the house."

Sandra wrung the soaking wet towels in the sink. "What happened?"

"I have no idea." Beside her, her mother wrung another towel then tossed it back on the still wet floor. "One minute I was grinding lemon rinds in the disposal and the next minute water was everywhere."

At that moment, the water boiling in a pan on the stove bubbled over.

"Lord, love a duck." Her mother sighed and standing closer, Sandra flipped the knob, turning off the gas. "Why don't you check on David? I'll finish the tea, then dry the rest of the floor."

Torn between the disaster on the first floor, and her son not feeling well upstairs, Sandra must have hesitated a moment too long for her mother's taste.

"Go. I'll get more towels."

"I'll check on David and bring the towels from our bathroom down."

"Sounds like a plan." Her mother sighed as she poured the green apple and lemon rind tea into a mug.

Taking the stairs two at a time, she made it to their room just in time to hear David retching through the closed door. "Marvelous." Hurrying into the room, her heart did a slow stutter at the miserable expression on her son's face. Poor kid was staring horrified at the mess on the blankets in front of him. At least most of his pajamas had been spared. "Oh, baby."

It didn't take long to change David out of his slightly soiled jammies and settle him into her bed—with a trash can—and strip the sheets from his bed.

"Here we go." Her mother came into the room with a

small tray, carrying the mug of tea and a dish of dry saltines. "We'll drink the tea first and if you get hungry, we can have some saltines, but not for at least an hour."

"You stay with him a few minutes and I'll run these sheets down to the laundry."

"Good idea."

The sheets bundled into a massive ball, she carried them in her arms, making her way down the stairs. Not quite to the bottom, the doorbell sounded. "Who the heck could that be?"

Some days simply dragged by, today was one of those days. Paxton had felt like a teen anticipating a first date with the head cheerleader. If he'd been unable to get Sandra out of his mind before, knowing they were going on a dinner date tonight kept her in the forefront of his mind. Even when he had to help out in the barn, not even hanging with the horses was enough to make him forget about Sandra.

Rather than waste time pretending to have something else that mattered, he opted to just accept that he was anxious and even a little nervous and might as well just give up and head to town. Having stopped to pick up some flowers, he hoped they would make an acceptable peace offering for arriving over an hour early.

Standing on her front porch, he picked one heck of a time to second-guess his decision. "Don't be stupid," he chastised himself. He could toss back and forth if arriving early was a blessing or an intrusion, but he was here, and if he didn't ring the darn bell, any minute now the neighbors would start a new topic of discussion on the grapevine. Taking a deep breath to steady his nerves, he rang the bell.

When the door flew open, a frazzled Sandra, loaded down with laundry, opened her mouth, then at the sight of him, snapped it shut. He couldn't be sure but he thought he heard her groan. Not a good sign.

"I came to town early and hoped that would be okay."

She sighed heavily. "David's sick and I need to wash his sheets." The last word had barely crossed her lips when the load slipped from her hands.

"Here." He reached forward. "Let me help."

"They're dirty."

He chuckled and pulled the linens from her arms. "That's usually what happens when someone's sick."

"I suppose you can leave them in the laundry room."

"If you tell me where it is I can go ahead and run the load while you go check on David."

"Mom's with him, and I can't have you doing our laundry."

"Nonsense." He smiled. "I've been doing laundry since I was ten years old. Mom insisted we all learn."

"But—"

"I got this. Show me the way then go check on..." his words evaporated when he found himself sloshing through puddles on the floor. "What the heck happened here?"

"Good question. From what I saw and Mom said, the disposal is possessed by devil spirits."

That had Paxton struggling to bite back a laugh. None of this was a laughing matter. "Go. I'll do the laundry."

"I can't—"

"Please."

Heaving a deep sigh, her shoulders slumped. "Okay. Fine. Washer's over there." She pointed to the hall beside the kitchen and turned to run upstairs.

The hours he'd spent imagining how tonight would go, doing laundry and fixing a possessed disposal had not crossed his mind, and yet, he was glad he'd come early. The laundry was in the washer and he found a mop and bucket and quickly began cleaning some of the mess. He'd wrung the wet towels out in the kitchen sink and set them on the dryer for the next load of wash. By the time Sandra's mother walked into the kitchen, he was under the sink.

"Oh, my."

"What's wrong?" Sandra came in on her mother's heels.

"Your dishwasher was backing into the disposal. Fixed the problem." He pushed to his feet and ran the water for a quick check, then turned back to the gaping woman. "How's David?"

"Asleep," Sandra spoke softly, taking in the room, her gaze settling on a couple of paper bags on the table.

"I thought, with David sick, you won't want to go out, and with an exploding sink, I doubted anyone had time to cook dinner, so I called Jamison and had him deliver some corned beef and cabbage meals with extra bread."

"You cleaned up the kitchen," Sandra muttered.

Paxton shrugged. "Mom taught us how to use a mop too."

The buzzer rang and Sandra and her mom looked toward the laundry room.

"That's the bed linens. They need to go in the dryer." He started toward the washer when Sandra's mom grabbed his arm.

"I've got it from here. You two eat." She smiled at him. "And thank you."

"My pleasure."

Moving slowly toward the cabinets, Sandra Lynn pulled out three dishes and then from a drawer pulled out some silverware. Her movements were slow and measured and Paxton feared he'd gone too far and now she was annoyed with him.

"I'm sorry if I overstepped, but it looked like y'all needed help."

Carrying the dishes and silverware to the kitchen table, she set it all down and turned to face him. "We did. Thank you."

He wished she sounded more convinced.

Slowly setting out each dish and adding the silverware, she shook her head and then looked up at him. "Anyone ever told you that you'd make a great knight in shining armor?"

"Can't say that they have." He opened the brown bags.

"Okay." Her mother appeared in the kitchen. "Linens are in the dryer, towels in the washer. I, for one, have had a very long day. I'm going to bed early tonight. You kids enjoy the food."

"You feeling okay?" Worry danced in Sandra's eyes.

"Perfectly fine for someone who wrestled a wayward disposal. I had a late lunch and am ready to just collapse on the sheets."

Sandra nodded. "Sleep well, Mom."

"Love you." She kissed her daughter's cheek and continued upstairs.

A moment later they were sitting across from each other enjoying O'Faredeigh's delicious food. Deciding that a little levity was required, Paxton brought up the time that Aunt Eileen came after the kids with a hose when she'd overheard one of the older cousins spewing inappropriate words for anyone except a truck driver.

"That really was funny." The twinkle returned to Sandra's eyes. "Especially when Adam went sliding across the muddy ground. It was like watching a show with the Three Stooges."

"It was definitely memorable."

"Thank you." Her smile softened. "You really came through for us. I appreciate it more than you know."

"I'm glad I could help, but sorry I didn't get here sooner for the disposal."

She shook her head. "You got here just in time. Thank you again."

"You're going to have to stop saying that. I was glad I could help. But I do want you to keep in mind that any time you or your mom are having trouble you can call me." He took a chance and placed his hand over hers. "I mean it."

Her gaze leveled with his. She seemed to be studying him as she processed his words, then finally nodded. "I believe you do."

CHAPTER THIRTEEN

Standing in the driveway of what would soon be Sandra Lynn's home, Paxton placed his tools in the bed of his truck, then stretched his aching muscles, twisting and turning from side to side. A couple of the crew had called in sick, so he'd strapped on his tool belt and worked inside today with his brothers and several of the volunteers.

Straightening, he turned to gaze at the house and caught Sandra standing on what would be the front walk, her hands on her hips, making similar stretching movements as he'd just done, her gaze never leaving the home. Not wanting to disturb her, he leaned against his truck and indulged in admiring her for a moment. One quality he admired in anyone was hard work, and Sandra had proven herself to be a very hard worker. Not only did she work all morning at the Cut n' Curl, she came to the job site every day, even when it wasn't required of her, and then she'd go home and care for her son and help her mother.

His mind wandered to last night. She worked so well under pressure. His mother would have been barking at everyone. Not that she didn't love her boys as much as Sandra Lynn did, but his mother tended to frazzle easily. Sandra Lynn stayed perfectly calm under pressure. Probably got that from her mother. The woman was sopping wet from dealing with the sink and then had pitched in to help with her sick grandson. He'd never been happier to lend an assist in his life. He just hoped the disposal didn't revolt again.

Unable to stay by his truck any longer without someone noticing, he strolled up to where she stood. "What do you think?"

Her hands dropping to her side, she turned a thousand-watt smile to him. "It's coming along great. Even better than I envisioned."

"Yeah?" Why did that make him want to puff out his chest like the proverbial peacock? After all, it wasn't as if he'd done all this single-handedly. "Construction Cousins do good work."

"You Farradays do it right. I think this house will be better built than any house in the county. Maybe in the whole country."

Although he and his brothers had healthy egos, even he wasn't prepared to think that much of himself. "I might give you county, perhaps even town, but definitely will be the best house on the block."

"So you have a modest side. Good to remember."

No one had ever called him modest before.

Her gaze shifted back to the house. "Ed would let me dream of our own home, but eventually I figured out it was just that, a dream."

"I gather your ex liked living in an apartment?"

"I suspect what he really liked was no maintenance. He wasn't one to enjoy hard work. Or any work." She bit her lip as if she'd revealed a deep dark secret.

The temptation to ask more about her ex pricked at him, but what little he knew about David's father already didn't sit well, he was afraid if he learned more, he would only want to strangle the guy. If there was a God in heaven, Paxton would never get the chance to encounter the jerk.

Dragging his thoughts away from a man he may not have met, but who he strongly disliked, he shifted his thoughts to Sandra's new home. "One good thing about a well-constructed new house, there won't be any repairs, at least not for a few years."

"I've been reading up on ordinary maintenance. I've already started looking for lawn mowers at garage sales. Might have to expand my shopping to Butler Springs."

"You know, there are plenty of people here in town to help you with ordinary maintenance and upkeep." He took a step closer and resisted the urge to run his finger down the side of that pretty face and promise her she'd never have to worry about overgrown lawns, leaky faucets or even a burned-out light bulb again. "That includes me."

Her smile softened and some of the sadness that had lingered in her gaze a few moments ago faded. "Thank you, but I need to learn how to do things for myself. I need to set the example for David. I see a lot of YouTube videos in my future."

Paxton chuckled. "Except those won't help much when water is spraying all over the place."

Shuddering, she groaned. "And don't I know that for a fact."

"Maybe we'll have to have a few Home Ownership 101 classes for you."

Her cheeks pinkened, and she smiled sweetly at him. "I'd like that."

Unsure of what to do or say next, he figured there was safety in retreat. "Listen, the day is done a little early, and Jamison serves the best buffalo wings during happy hour. I mean, it's not the dinner I owe you, but can I tempt you anyway?"

Bobbing her head, she pulled out her phone and typed in a text. Before she could look up, her phone dinged with a response. A few more taps on the phone and her smile grew brighter as she tucked the phone back into her pocket. "Now I'm free."

O'Faredeigh's was halfway between the construction site and her mother's. It only took a couple of minutes to arrive. He pulled into the space by the front door. The tunes from the jukebox wafted over from across the family pub. If he was lucky, maybe he could talk Sandra into a dance. A legitimate reason to hold her close.

"Hey Paxton." Wearing a white apron tied around his waist, Jamison came out from behind the bar. "Didn't expect to see you in here so early. Thought y'all would still be working at the house."

"Called it a day early." His gaze darted away from his cousin in search of where Sandra had continued walking.

"How's the project coming along?"

"Great. With all the help we've had, we're way ahead

of schedule." He spotted Sandra stopped at a nearby table, chatting and smiling with a woman, he figured it must be someone she knew. Of course, in a town this size, everyone pretty much knew everyone.

Jamison turned his head, his gaze following the same direction as Paxton's. "You'd better go rescue Sandra. Katie is nice enough, but her brother is a bit of a prick. Thinks he's God's gift to women and after a few beers, he gets a little handsy."

Handsy? Paxton didn't like the sound of that at all. Not one little bit.

While Sandra had lived away from home, life in Tuckers Bluff had seemed so far away and so long ago. Now, as people she knew called to her, she felt as if she'd never left home, and once again she thanked heaven that she'd come home. Surprised by the crowd at such an early hour, Sandra spotted several empty tables and attempted to cross the room to one in the far corner of the room. What could she say, she wanted some semblance of privacy for her time with Paxton.

"Sandra, hey," Katie, one of her former classmates, grabbed her arm. "I heard you were back in town."

Even though Katie had never been one of her favorite people, Sandra gave the woman a smile. "Hi."

"You need a seat? You by yourself?" Katie shoved the guy beside her over and patted the seat beside her.

Sandra glanced over at Paxton talking by the door with his cousin. "I'm with someone, but thanks for asking."

It took another moment for her to recognize Katie's brother at her side. Another person she'd never cared for in high school. Former football player, and as dumb and annoying as the stereotypical jock. The guy looked around and turning his attention back to Sandra, what was supposed to be a smile looked more like a sneer. "One drink. It'll be fun."

She shook her head. "I really want to snag a table before they're all gone." She faced Katie again. "We'll have to catch up another time."

"Of course." Katie's smile seemed sincere. Maybe she'd turned out to be a nice person, but tonight wasn't the time to find out.

Before she could fully back away from the table, Paxton appeared at her side and slid his hand onto her lower back. "I see a table over there."

She nodded at him, waved her fingers at Katie, ignored her brother, and as they walked, turned to face him. "Thank you."

"For what?" His hand was still at her back as they approached the same table she'd spied a few minutes ago.

"Saving me from having to talk any longer to Katie and her brother." Had she been here with Ed, the man would have completely ignored her as long as he had a full drink to make love to. She tried not to think about how much time she wasted. Being here with Paxton made standing tall, and feeling safe, easy.

"Any time." Stopping at the small table and pulling out her chair, he smiled at her. "I mean that."

Somehow, she was sure he really did. "Knowing everyone in the place is part of the price of living in a small town. And I freely admit, a price I'll gladly pay for David to have a safe place to grow up. Though in your case, you're probably related to more than half of the people here."

Quickly, he glanced around, and nodded. "That's a fair estimate."

A soft melody played on the juke box and Sandra found herself swaying in her seat as she read the menu on the table.

"You still like to dance?"

Her eyes popped open and she stopped swaying. A flash of memory struck her. She and Grace and Hannah and Becky at the Farraday ranch, in the family room with the music playing and the four of them, having already moved all the furniture out of the way, line dancing. The recollection made her chuckle. "Yes, I guess I do."

A waitress came to the table. "What can I get you, Paxton?"

"Hey, Sara." He waved for Sandra to go first, then he ordered a drink and some wings. "Do you like fried mushrooms?"

She bobbed her head. Her mother often lovingly teased, calling her a cow. *You don't eat girl, you graze.*

The waitress walked away, promising to be back with their drinks, and he pushed his seat away from the table and extended his hand to her. "Shall we?"

Immediately, her gaze darted around the place. "No one else is dancing?"

He shrugged. "Someone has to be the first."

Right. Someone. She'd be an idiot to say no. This was her chance to get close to him. Really close. Unable to make the words come out of her mouth, she simply smiled and nodded.

A popular country tune had them falling into an easy Texas Two-Step.

"You're a good dancer." She almost giggled as he spun her around before pulling her into him again.

"Mom said it was the best way to get girls. That or learn to play the piano. Dancing seemed easier."

"I'll have to remember that. Make sure to teach David to dance."

He stared at her a long moment before spinning her out and bringing her back again. "You'd do anything for David, wouldn't you?"

"Absolutely. Not only is he my world right now, but that's what being a parent is all about. You bring this helpless child into the world who you have to teach how not to be helpless."

He seemed to consider her words before nodding. "I never thought about it that way. Kind of brings home what a huge responsibility it is having children."

"Every decision I make, I have to think about David, how it will affect him. Will it make his life better or worse."

"I hope I fall into the category of better."

Her smile widened. "Absolutely. You're an amazing

influence on him. And it doesn't hurt that he adores you."

"Nah." Paxton chuckled. "The kid just likes me for my pitching arm and the horses."

Her head tipped back with laughter. "There's that too."

"Seriously, though, I hope you know that I would never do anything to bring any harm to David."

Oh, how she wished David's own father had felt that way. Putting David first or considering him in any decision was not on her ex's radar. "I do."

He spun them around and seemed to hold her a smidge closer than a moment before. If only Paxton had returned to Tuckers Bluff for more summer vacations. Would they have stayed friends? Become something more? Would David be his son, not Ed's? Shoulda, woulda, coulda. Instead of lingering on what might have or could have been, what she needed to learn was to enjoy the here and now. And from where she stood at the moment, the here and now was looking awfully bright.

CHAPTER FOURTEEN

The last thing Paxton needed was for the film crew to be here today. At least for now, they were off in the master bedroom filming Sandra and Ryan taping and bedding the sheetrock, getting it ready for adding texture. Sandra had become really good at it. So much so, that Ryan even told her if she ever wanted to give up working in a beauty salon, she could have a job on the construction crew. That had Paxton smiling. The lady was truly a cut above the rest. He'd thought so when they were kids, and he still thought so.

"You forget how to measure?" Quinn stepped up beside him.

"Of course not."

Dark brows folded into a frown. "So there's a good reason you cut the sheetrock too short?"

"What?" He drilled the last screw into the sheetrock he was hanging and turned to his brother.

Quinn pointed to the sheet he'd laid against the wall where Paxton worked. The one he was supposed to screw in next. Also, the one that clearly wasn't long enough to reach the end of the wall. How the heck had this happened? The fifteen foot wall was a foot shorter than the two pieces of sheet rock. He knew that, yet somehow he'd gotten eighteen inches stuck in his head and he'd cut the boards too short.

"Guess I was a bit distracted."

"Distracted?" The frown between Quinn's brows deepened. "What gives?"

No way he was going to tell his brother that he'd had dinner and dancing with Sandra on his mind. They'd had such a good time, talking, laughing, and dancing. The dancing, of course, was his favorite. A legitimate excuse to hold her close, and once other patrons joined them on the floor, it was easy to simply blend in. If he closed his eyes, he could almost still feel Sandra swaying in his arms. And *that* was probably how he mucked up the measuring.

The lights from the filming crew dimmed in the distance. One by one they came out of the back of the house, smiling, chatting, and waving at Paxton as they walked by and tossing departing words of encouragement at Sandra. It made no sense, but it bothered him that everyone seemed to like her so much.

"You contemplating the immortality of the crab?" Quinn crossed his arms.

"Why's this not done?" Ryan walked into the room that he'd expected to find all the sheetrock up. "Guess I'd better help or we'll fall behind."

Shaking his head, Quinn dropped his arms by his side and turned to Ryan. "Just for the hell of it, show him how to use a tape measure."

Ryan looked from one brother to the other, his mouth hanging slightly open, utter confusion covered his face.

"Don't ask." Paxton sighed, and smiled at Sandra approaching.

"Hey." She stopped in front of him.

He resisted the urge to reach out and hug her or take her hand or just run a finger down that soft cheek. But the workplace was not the place for public displays of affection. "You look like the cat that swallowed the canary."

"Something like that." Her shoulders hitched with excitement. "My license came through and Polly says I can have afternoon appointments since Margie, her regular manicurist, only works mornings."

While he considered what this meant for their workday, she flung herself at him, throwing her arms around his neck. He'd barely wrapped his arms around her waist in a return hug when she tensed and took a step in retreat. Her cheeks flushing a soft pink, and her head dipped, she glanced over at Ryan busying himself with the sheetrock on the opposite wall. "Sorry about that."

He shook his head. "Nonsense, this is good news for you." No point in mentioning that he wished he could have held her longer.

"The downside is that I won't be able to work on the house every day. Do you think that will be a problem?"

He leaned back against the doorjamb. "That should be fine. You already work here more than you need to. You've banked enough hours of sweat equity that you could never show up again and you'd still get the house."

Her eyes lit up. "You guys look at it that way?"

"Not us, the charity."

"That's nice, but I still feel like a slacker if I don't show up at all."

"Don't even think about it. All is fine. Though we'll miss you."

"We?" she teased.

"I'm sure everyone here has enjoyed working with you, but I'll definitely miss having you around."

"You will?"

He bobbed his head and his heart did a two-step when her smile blossomed. "Is it awful of me to say I'm glad?"

"Not even a little." He shook his head.

"I'm going to miss being here too."

That had his cheeks tugging at the corners of his mouth. "I'm glad to hear that."

"You two going to get back to work or keep up the grinning competition?" Quinn muttered on his way through the room toward the door without slowing or saying anything further.

Stepping further apart, he briefly considered pulling her into his arms and dipping her for a dramatic kiss just to tick off his grumpy brother, but decided that would be opening a can of worms that could seriously backfire. For now, he was going to have to keep his hands—and lips—to himself.

Sandra could still feel the warmth of that too-brief hug from a few minutes ago. She hadn't meant to hug him in front of everyone, but she was just so darn excited. "This means I'll be able to save even more money for furniture and what not when the house is finally ready."

"Working full time will help, I'm sure."

"Absolutely. And if it's slow, I can still do shampoos. Tips aren't as good for shampooing as for doing manicures and pedicures, but money is money."

"My mother always said, a little of something is better than all of nothing."

Her mother often said something very similar. Hopefully, it would all be enough.

"Hey, where did that bubbly enthusiasm just go?" He took a step closer and seemed to think better of it and rocked back on his boot heels.

"Margie has her regulars, so I'll have to build my own following. That may take a little time. I know there's only one salon in Tuckers Bluff but having Margie work mornings only seemed to be good enough till now."

"I'm sure it will work out. All you need is for word of mouth to spread and all will be well. You'll see. When do you start?"

She glanced at her watch. "In an hour."

"Oh." His eyes widened slightly and then his smile reappeared. "Break a leg."

Biting back a giggle, she smiled at him. "I don't know if that works in the beauty business the same as in show business, but thanks."

With a quick peck on the cheek and a wave to Ryan and the others, she was out the door on her way home for a quick lunch. Shoveling down a peanut butter and jelly sandwich, between bites she told her mother what little she knew.

"Don't you worry. There's plenty more people in Tuckers Bluff who want to get their nails done. They'll learn Polly has more help and come. Like that movie. If you build it, they will come."

That had her chuckling with her last swallow. "Paxton said something similar. But I want to get there early today."

She jumped to her feet and kissed her mother on the cheek. "I'm leaving. See you for dinner."

"Unless Paxton invites you out again," her mom called over her shoulder.

Rolling her eyes at no one in particular, she ran out the door and practically skipped to the salon. To her surprise, Polly had found the room to add a second nail station. Sandra had assumed that she'd be using Margie's station, but somehow, knowing she had her own spot made today even more exciting. Putting away her purse in the bottom drawer, even though she had no standing appointments, she proceeded to set the table up in preparation for her first customer.

Sorting through nail files and clippers, and taking note of a few items she'd like to have than what Polly had provided, she made a mental note to order some specialty polishes that lasted longer than the average manicure. She'd brought a few from home, but needed a wider selection. Completely set up and organized, she wondered what to do next when the bell over the door sounded.

Meg Farraday hurried through the door. "Sorry I'm a little late. Had a guest arrive early for check in as I was walking out the door. Is it too late?"

Holding a woman's long hair between her fingers, and a pair of scissors primed to snip off a long lock, Polly smiled. "Right on time."

Sandra looked at the woman who had married Adam Farraday right around the same time she had married Ed. The difference, of course, was that Meg had married a good man and had a lovely and very happy family. Expecting Meg to wait for Polly or another of the stylists, Sandra was surprised to see her plop in the seat in front of her.

"My nails are such a mess. It's so hard to chase after a little one, care for guests, and keep my nails polished. I swear, a few days out and my nails look like hell and break like there's no tomorrow."

Sandra pointed to her specialty polishes. "I don't have many color choices yet, but I'll be getting more soon." For the next few minutes, she explained the benefits of this polish over ordinary and was halfway through the manicure when Connor Farraday's wife Catherine came through the door.

The woman waved at Polly, stopped to chat with Ida Brady in Polly's chair a moment before, all smiles, grabbed the chair at Margie's station and pulled it over to her sister-in-law. "Isn't this fun having someone available in the afternoons for a manicure?"

Meg leaned forward and looked at her hands. "It's heaven."

Sandra smelled a rat. Or at least a little mouse.

The two sisters-in-law talked colors, and schedules, and children before circling around to the women's Friday night Girls' Night.

"We do hope you can make it some time." Admiring her nails, Meg switched places with Catherine.

The two women were still chatting when Grace was the next person through the front door. There was no doubt in Sandra's mind that this wasn't a coincidence. Not once in the weeks she'd been working here had any of these women come in for a haircut so having all three here for manicures definitely smelled of a rat. A sweet and thoughtful rat.

Unlike the other two women, Grace's polish was still intact, her hands looked smooth and fresh, and Sandra would bet her old friend had recently had a manicure.

Cordless phone in hand, Polly stopped by Sandra's station. "I have someone on the phone who wants an appointment later today. Are you open or do you expect another client?"

Wouldn't she like to know? She almost felt like calling Paxton to ask him if he had any more family he was sending her way. "I think I'm free. Who wants an appointment?"

"Eileen Farraday."

Yep. She was definitely going to need to have a little chat with Paxton Farraday.

CHAPTER FIFTEEN

One of the perks of running your own company and not being part of the construction crew but the landscape team, meant Paxton could leave the job site any time he wanted. In this case, he wanted to leave in time to surprise Sandra Lynn after her first day of work.

Leaned against the wall between the Cut n' Curl and the new craft store, he glanced at his watch. She should be done any moment. He'd gotten a text from his cousin Grace that even though Sandra didn't say anything, every time a Farraday walked in the door with a last-minute nail appointment, she gave them a funny look. A look that got more intense with each arrival.

Quickly realizing his mistake, he reached out to Adam and had him send his younger vet tech over on his dime as an employee perk. Thankfully, all the Farradays had a soft spot for Sandra Lynn, because of her situation they were even more interested in helping out. Somehow, the tech had been delighted to participate and maneuvered Adam into both a manicure and pedicure. Tomorrow, he'd talk to Brooks. There had to be a slew of ladies at his clinic who he could give an employee manicure for a bonus. Though, now that he thought about it, Aunt Eileen was most likely already working on setting up every female in town to go support Sandra Lynn. He'd have to talk to her tonight before he did anything else.

The front door squeaked open and Sandra's voice floated onto the street. "Thanks again, Polly. See you tomorrow."

"It was a great day, Sandra Lynn," Polly answered, a contented lilt to her voice.

"So it went well?" Paxton eased away from the wall.

Sandra gasped and jumped back a foot. "Didn't anyone ever tell you not to sneak up on someone?"

"I wasn't sneaking." He gave her his best *aren't I irresistible* smile.

"Close enough." She shook her head at him, and was not smiling back. "You scared the dickens out of me."

"Sorry. I didn't mean to. I was just anxious to find out how your day went and see if I could talk you into telling me all about it over dinner?"

Still standing in front of the salon doorway, her foot barely tapping, she speared him with a studious glare. "On one condition."

He bobbed his head.

"You agree to tell me the truth, the whole truth, and nothing but the truth."

Uh-oh. Did he have a choice? "Agreed."

The smile he so had gotten used to and loved seeing, took over her face. "Walk with me. Mom's birthday is this weekend and I made enough in tips today to do a little shopping at Sisters."

"Really?" He hoped his expression displayed innocence and not triumph.

"You know darn well I had a busy day."

"I do?"

Her steps slowed, and she turned her head to face him. "Truth, the whole truth, and nothing but the truth."

He blew out a sigh. "Okay, maybe I had an idea you might be a bit busy."

"Might?"

"There are a lot of people in this town."

"And all of them suddenly needed a manicure this afternoon?" She was still smiling so any irritation she might have initially held at his interference was hopefully gone.

"Did they?"

Again, she stopped in her tracks, and hands on her hips, twisted to face him. Her silence yelled at him louder than any words.

"Okay. I guess they did."

Her smile back again, she leaned in and kissed his cheek. "Thank you."

"You're not angry at me?"

"Well." She rocked back on her heels. "Maybe a little at first, but it was easier not sitting alone waiting for someone to come in. I was so busy that I couldn't even help with the shampooing."

"Good." He continued walking to the sister's store. "I know that once more folks in town learn that Polly has an afternoon manicurist, business will boom."

"The Farradays seemed to be doing that single-handedly."

That made him chuckle. "Well, you have to admit, there are a lot of us."

"Can't argue with that. Just since I left Tuckers Bluff, your Oklahoma clan is back, and half of them are married." She chuckled softly. "Hard to believe so many of us who ran around together as kids, joking, and playing, and laughing ourselves to death over any silly thing from mud pies to water fights, most of us have kids of our own doing the same things."

From time to time, when there were a bunch of little ones running around at the ranch, even though none of them were his, he felt the same way. How the heck had that happened? When did they all grow up? And then he'd wonder if he and Quinn and Ryan would find someone to make them as happy as his other brothers and cousins were. Not a single one in the bunch had chosen poorly. The whole blasted family seemed to be excruciatingly happy. Something he loved seeing.

Reaching the boutique, he stepped to one side and opened the door for her. "Here we are."

With a bright grin, she bobbed her head, softly said, *yes we are*, and walked past him. His chest tightened, and his breath hitched. As sure as he knew his name was Paxton Farraday, he hoped he was as sure that her short response had nothing to do with the store and everything to do with them. Oh, how he hoped.

The bell over the Sisters door announced their arrival and Sissy the tall redheaded sibling came hurrying out from behind the curtain, a surprisingly harsh expression on her face and marching like a soldier prepared to do battle. The second her gaze landed on them, her shoulders eased, her steps grew lighter and a smile bloomed. "Oh, thank heavens it's you."

Worried, Sandra quickly glanced at Paxton before turning back to face Sissy. "Is something wrong? Do you need help?"

"Oh, no." The woman waved a hand at them. "We just had the surliest customer."

"Surly is being nice." Sister came out from the curtain. "I have never had to count to ten so many times in one shopping experience in my life."

"Now, now, Sister." Sissy patted her sister on the arm. "Let's say our prayers that he's just passing through."

"I'll agree to that," the short blonde with a hairdo as big as she was, nodded. "We need people with that attitude moving to our town like we need holes in our heads."

"Should I be calling Declan?" Paxton's gaze had narrowed, clearly worried about the two older women enough to call his cousin the police chief. His concern for others made Sandra's heart swell. No matter how hard she told herself to remember they were friends and she had no business getting involved with another man, she was most definitely getting involved, and things like this were making it all too easy to fall hard for Paxton Farraday.

Both sisters shook their heads.

Sister sighed. "It's not like he did anything illegal but I swear that man did not have one nice word to say about a single thing in this shop. All he did was grumble about poor selection, low quality, and high prices."

"I told him we pride ourselves on carrying the best items at the lowest possible price." Sissy was getting red-faced just retelling the situation. "But that didn't stop him one bit from finding fault with every last thing he touched."

"And he touched a lot." Sister had moved over to straighten displays and refold items.

Sandra suspected the items she'd been arranging had been ones the unpleasant customer had touched and moved. "At least he's gone now." When she turned to Paxton she noticed him by the window, looking down both sides of the street.

Apparently so did Sister. "I'm sure he's long gone."

"And if we're lucky," Sissy added, "already out of town with no intention of coming back."

"Still." Paxton turned back to the women. "Next time the customer might not be just mean-spirited but could have something else up his sleeve. I want you to promise you'll call Declan or any one of us who are nearby when a customer like that comes in."

"Don't be silly," Sissy waved him off.

"I'm not. The world is changing and just because Tuckers Bluff is a peaceful friendly place doesn't mean the ways of the world can't touch us."

The two sisters frowned, tight lipped. Then Sister nodded. "There were those idiot dog smugglers who tried to kidnap Valerie, and then that rapist in Butler Springs not so long ago."

Sissy nodded too. "And remember the time poor Jake Thomas took his wife and Meg hostage. Someone could have been killed."

Placing her hand on Sissy's arm, Sister shook her head. "Now, that's not the same thing. He had a brain tumor. Can't blame the way the world is changing on him."

"True." Sissy nodded and then, as if someone had snapped them out of their thoughts, her bright smile reappeared. "I'm sure we'll be fine, but we do promise if another mean-spirited customer like that comes in again, we'll call Declan."

Paxton looked to Sister.

The woman smiled at him. "We both agree."

"Good." He pivoted to face Sandra. He sure hoped that talk of smugglers, kidnapping, rapists, and hostages didn't change her mind about moving back to Tuckers Bluff. Through no fault of his own, he'd lost touch with her once, he didn't know much about her coming home yet, but he did know one thing for sure; he did not want to lose touch again.

CHAPTER SIXTEEN

The low hum of dinner conversation from the Silver Spur Café hit Paxton as the old-fashioned bell chimed above them. At least without the music, the café would be more conducive to conversation than O'Faredeigh's. Talking—and hearing—would be much easier here, and that's what he really wanted, to hear firsthand everything about how Sandra's afternoon had gone.

Abbie, the owner of the diner and his cousin Jamison's wife, waved them to a booth at the opposite side of the cafe. Thankful for any opportunity to be close, he placed his hand at the small of Sandra's back and guided her past the tables and booths. Of course, half the dinner guests recognized them, delaying their efforts with the polite chitchat.

Sliding into opposite sides of the booth, Paxton set his hat down beside him, while Sandra reached for the menu. The thing about Abbie's café is that most of the folks in town knew every item and didn't bother with menus. That Sandra reached for one reminded him of just how long she'd been gone.

"You aren't going to look, are you?" She glanced at him from over the top of the menu.

"Took me a few weeks to memorize it like the rest of the locals, but once I did, it actually made everything feel more like home."

Bobbing her head, Sandra looked back at her menu and then glanced up at him again. "I'm noticing not much has changed. Hopefully, I won't need weeks to fall back into local mode."

He liked the sound of that. There were a lot of things he

was liking right about now. Sandra being at the top of his list.

Abbie stopped at the booth, her pad in her hand. "How do you like being home?"

"I love it." Sandra's gaze shifted a moment to Paxton and he'd have sworn he saw her blush. Was he reading something into her response? Or maybe it was just wishful thinking.

"Glad to hear." Abbie gave that same comforting smile that made all her customers love dining at the café. "Your mom was in here earlier with your son."

"Really?"

"After school ice cream sundae."

Sandra smiled, rolling her eyes. "Gotta love grandmas."

"What a delight your son is. He's a great kid."

Sandra beamed. "Thank you."

"I'm not an expert on kids," Paxton chimed in, "but I think he's pretty great too."

"You do?" Sandra's brows buckled.

He merely nodded but had to wonder why she looked so surprised.

"Yeah," Abbie grinned, "he told me some jokes and I laughed at all of them."

"I didn't know my son was such a comedian," Sandra said.

"Indeed." Abbie tapped her pad. "So, what can I get you folks?"

Paxton motioned for Sandra to go first.

"Does Frank still make the best cheeseburger this side of the Mississippi?"

"He sure does." Abbie nodded.

"Great. Cheeseburger with Swiss cheese, tomatoes, on whole wheat with sweet potato fries."

Abbie looked to Paxton. "I'll have the same," he said.

With a smile and nod of her head, Abbie left them to return promptly with their drinks.

Dipping the straw in and out of her cola, Sandra leveled her gaze with his. "I wonder where David gets his sense of humor from?"

The question seemed a little odd to him. Sandra seemed to have a good sense of humor, but she wasn't a big jokester. "Maybe it's just a kid thing?"

She shrugged her shoulders. "Maybe."

"I gather neither you nor his father are big on joke telling?"

Sandra shook her head. "I might tell a joke or two every once in a while, but there wasn't really anything funny about Ed." A frown took over her face.

Not the reaction he wanted. It was pretty clear that Sandra's ex-husband was still a sore spot in her life. He didn't know what had happened, and didn't want to pry, but despite his curiosity, he opted to change the subject. "Tell me about your afternoon."

"Anyone would think Polly's salon had a revolving door. I was busy pretty much all afternoon. But you already know that."

All he did was smile. He knew how important this job was to her and the few women in the family who he'd managed to get the word out to had been more than happy to pitch in and help Sandra out.

A wistful look crossed her face. "I have to admit, it's nice to be in a place where I am appreciated."

Another waitress appeared, set their order in front of them, and Paxton studied Sandra Lynn as she smiled down at her burger. Questions about her life continued to taunt him. He so desperately wanted to wipe away all the painful memories, but last time he looked, no one had died and made him God. Which left him only one choice, help keep that smile on her face.

Drawing the napkin across his lap, he reached for his burger. "Then it sounds like moving home is a good start."

Swallowing her first bite, she nodded. "When I was a kid, growing up where everyone and their grandmother knew everything about you, and made it a point to share it with your parents, was horribly off-putting. The outside world looked so much more appealing. I thought Ed was my ticket to seeing the world. Enjoying things not available in Tuckers Bluff. By the time we ended the marriage, I felt more isolated than I ever did in a small town. You could say I learned my lesson about what really matters. Now, the idea of going out to dinner where someone shares things your son did, or spreads the word about your new job, all of that is enormously comforting."

"I think that's why my brothers and I are all happily settling in here in Tuckers Bluff instead of Oklahoma."

"If you don't mind my asking, why did y'all stop coming back to visit?"

Wasn't that the billion-dollar question? He shrugged. "We don't know. Mom told us that we weren't welcome anymore, and we believed her. Turns out, the family here had no idea why we stopped coming."

"That is odd." Sandra sat back in the booth, nibbling on the last of her fries. "For a little while there I wondered if it was something I'd done." She raised her hand before he could speak. "I know that was silly, but so many people were so stunned at your family's absence. Obviously, I quickly figured out that whatever it was, it was a lot bigger than me or anyone else around here."

"I loved my time here. And I have so many fond memories of racing horses across the fields, gigging frogs in the creek, hide and seek. And you."

Now her smile widened enough for her eyes to sparkle. "I missed you."

"Ditto." That shouldn't have made him as happy as it did, but he felt his heart swell and his cheeks tug at his smile and he wanted to crow like a rooster ready to announce the break of day.

As Abbie lifted the empty plates from the table, Sandra Lynn's phone dinged. "Sorry, I need to check in case it's about David."

"Of course." He drew his napkin across his lap and picked up the fork. Not at all happy to see her smile slip and her brows draw together in a tight V as she tossed her phone back into her purse.

Taking a sip of water, he wondered if she was going to say anything. Silence reigned heavily and he decided enough was enough. Pulling a few bills from his wallet and setting them on the table, he looked at her. "Let's take a walk?"

Dinner had been as much fun as every time she'd been with Paxton. Just having him near filled her with contentment. Even when her ex sent her cryptic texts, just knowing Paxton was there made things seem more palatable.

Holding the door for her, the second they crossed out of the café, Paxton reached for her hand. "Do you mind?"

Mind? Was he crazy? She suddenly felt fifteen years old when you'd look at the cutest boy in the class, your stomach started doing flip flops, and you spent every night hoping that just once, he'd notice you. "I don't mind at all."

"Thought we'd head over to the park. It's a short walk, but a nice evening."

She nodded and for the first time in a very long time, just enjoyed the fresh air and company. How long had it been since she'd relished a man's company? They reached the park and neither had a said a word. The sun was dipping behind the horizon and soon the stars would be shining big and bright, just like the song said.

"Shall we?" Still holding her hand, he gestured to the set of swing benches.

She gave a single nod and they eased onto the seat and Paxton lightly kicked it off so they were in a slow sway.

Delighted he had not let go of her hand, she twisted to face him. "Thanks for dinner. Again. Next time, though, my treat."

"We'll see."

The way he flashed that lopsided grin that made her want to smile right back; she knew he had no intention of letting her pay. Some people would call that attitude chauvinist or even controlling. Not her. As far as she was concerned, she loved good old-fashioned chivalry. Having Paxton treat her like a lady.

They swung in silence for several minutes before

Paxton cleared his throat. "So, want to tell me about that text?"

Did she? It took her another moment to realize that she really did want to share with him. "Ed."

Paxton bobbed his chin, but let her speak at her own pace.

"Every so often I get texts where he's yelling at me for something."

Again, he nodded.

"This time he's lost another job. He missed a few days' work and got fired. He thinks it's my fault for leaving."

"How does your leaving cause him to lose time at work?"

Why was anything her fault? What was the point of protecting Ed anymore? "If I'm not there to wake him up, he'll sleep the day away. But it doesn't really matter. For him, everything he did wrong was always my fault."

All Paxton did was bite down on his back teeth. She had the feeling he wanted to say something but refrained.

"You see, shortly after David was born, Ed started drinking more. Nothing much. A few extra beers after work to unwind. Then he started drinking whisky. Said it helped him sleep through the baby crying all night."

Paxton blew out a heavy and disapproving sigh.

"By the time David was a toddler, Ed was drinking heavily from the minute he got home until he fell into bed. Literally. I kept telling myself that as long as he didn't drink during the day, it wasn't that bad. That may be, when David didn't need so much of my time, Ed would ease up on the booze."

"I gather that didn't happen?"

This time she shook her head. "I suspected he was taking something else during the day, but couldn't prove it. Eventually it got so bad that I had to practically drag him out of bed, fill him with coffee, and some mornings even dress him like a little kid."

She could see Paxton processing her words, and knew from the twitch in his jaw that he was struggling to keep calm and silent.

"After a couple more years I realized that the only thing keeping me in the marriage was my pride. So I filed for divorce."

"And he didn't fight you?"

"He was too drunk to keep his thoughts straight. But he did fight for full custody."

Paxton's eyes flew open wide as silver dollars.

"I always knew it wasn't for the love of his son, he hardly paid any attention to him at all. Last year, after a fight about his drinking, he grabbed David and stormed out of the house. I couldn't stop him, so I called the police. They wouldn't do anything about it. They patiently told me that it's not illegal for a man to go out with his son, even if the only time he ever took David anywhere was to get back at me for something. I was so scared."

"I'm so sorry you had to go through that." His hand landed on hers, giving her the strength to keep talking.

"Thankfully, because of his work records, one DUI, and my reporting him drunk and driving with David in the car, the judge agreed to shared custody only if Ed underwent regular drug testing. When he refused, that's when I knew I'd been right about him mixing drugs with alcohol. At that point the judge granted me permission to move home even though Texas was out of state. Ed was spitting mad, though I never understood why. He doesn't care about David. I don't know, maybe he really does hate me enough to take my son away from me. But," she forced a smile, "that's all over and now we're safe and sound in Tuckers Bluff."

It took Paxton a few moments to form words. "Thank you."

"Excuse me?"

"Thank you for trusting me with your story."

If it were physically possible for a heart to melt, hers would have. The man was thanking her. She sure was glad that somehow fate had managed to bring her and Paxton both back to Tuckers Bluff at the same time. For the first time in a long time, she felt as if everything was not just going to be better, it was going to be great. And there wasn't a thing Ed Morton could do to ruin it.

CHAPTER SEVENTEEN

It had taken everything in Paxton not to jump up and say a few choice words about Sandra's ex. This explained so much. Why David didn't seem to have any age appropriate skills that most boys learn from their dads, why the child never showed signs of missing his dad or wanting to see the man, and why Sandra Lynn too often seemed downright beaten down. Once or twice as she spoke, he'd wanted desperately to ask if the drunk had ever laid a hand on her but decided not to. He truly hoped not, or his brothers might have to strap him down to stop him from seeking the jerk out and tearing him to shreds, limb by limb.

"This was a nice idea." Still swinging, Sandra stared out at the gazebo in the middle of the park. "The town did a nice job with this park. It has something for both kids and adults alike."

That he could easily agree with. "They have summer picnics with bands playing in the gazebo. I've only been to a couple, but it's a ton of fun."

"I can see that."

"They have face painters, and those clowns who make balloon poodles. The kids love it. I bet David would have a blast."

"I think you're right. He laughs a lot more now. I like that."

"I'm sorry." It was all Paxton could think to say.

"I was stupid to expect Ed to change."

He shook his head. "Not stupid, hopeful. After all, you did love the man once."

"Maybe. I think I was in love with the dream he

promised, not so much the man. Though at the time, I didn't realize it."

"Dreams are hard to let go of."

"I suppose, but for the first time in a long time, it looks as though most of mine will come true. A sweet son, a house with a big yard for him and a dog."

"You want a dog?"

She nodded. "Definitely. Every little boy needs a dog."

His mind turned over to Gray at the ranch. A good dog like that would be perfect. He'd have to check around if any of Gray's offspring was having puppies.

"Speaking of which." Sandra glanced down at her watch. "It's getting late. Mom is probably getting David ready for bed, but I still should go home to at least kiss him goodnight."

"Of course." Without hesitation, he pushed to his feet. Not till he stood did he realize he had not for a single moment let go of Sandra's hand. He loved the feel of her delicate hand in his, but more so, loved that she had not once tried to pull away from him. Not till they'd reached his truck by the café did he release his hold on her. Closing the passenger door, he quickly circled the hood and climbed into the vehicle.

A short distance from her mother's, her phone dinged again and that same troubled frown appeared.

"Your ex again?"

She nodded.

"Does he usually reach out multiple times?"

Her head turned from side to side. "No." Still staring at the phone for another moment, she let the phone drop to her lap and her head fall back against the seat. "He wants to visit with David."

She'd been here for weeks already and this was the first he'd heard of David's father actually wanting to see his son. "Has he asked before?"

"No." She lifted the phone again and stared at the screen. "He didn't fuss when the judge gave me permission to move out of state. He seemed happy to exchange parental privileges to avoid paying support."

"He doesn't pay you?"

Again, her head turned from side to side. "Mom and I discussed it and we agreed that we would be better off raising David on our own than letting Ed disrupt his life in exchange for financial support."

"But he wants to see him anyway?"

"So much for no interest if it saves him money." On a deep sigh, she closed her eyes and let her head fall back against the seat. "I guess I'm going to have to pay a visit to Declan."

"Declan?" What did she need with his cousin, the police chief? Unless, the jerk really had been physical with her.

Turning her head to face him, she blew out another long sigh. "One of the conditions of visitations if Ed decided to see his son was that they had to be supervised."

Paxton's blood ran cold and his fingers tightened around the steering wheel. "Did he try to hurt David?"

"Other than driving drunk with him in the car, no." She opened her eyes again. "I guess I might as well tell you the rest of the story."

Biting down hard on his back teeth, he prepared himself for what he didn't want to hear.

"Ed got caught up in a police sting. He seems to have an affinity for high-school-aged girls. Or at least ones he thought were teens. In the middle of the custody hearing, he was caught with a young looking police woman who Ed thought was a high school girl looking for a little fun, as he called it."

Every minute this guy just kept piling on the reasons for Paxton to really want to ship this character off on a one-way passage to the moon.

"I have to let him visit, but it has to be supervised and honestly, I'd rather that be with someone who can make sure Ed doesn't do anything stupid."

"You don't think he'd hurt him, do you?" Not that Paxton was putting anything past this guy. He sounded like a typical controlling and emotional, if not physically abusive, spouse. Especially if it meant hurting Sandra through their son.

"He's a cowardly lush with a nasty mouth who thinks David ruined our marriage, but even so, sober, I don't think he'd do anything to him."

"What a moron." Oops, he hadn't meant to say that out loud. "Have you told Grace any of this?"

She shook her head.

"Might not be a bad idea to get a good lawyer involved as well. You know, just in case." Though he suspected, knowing his family, wherever David and his father met, there would be a whole heck of a lot of Farradays nearby to keep the guy on the straight and narrow. Including him.

Sandra didn't like the idea of too many people knowing what David's father was truly like. The last thing she wanted was for people to paint her son with the same brush. For just a moment, she gave herself pause. When had she stopped thinking of Ed as her husband—or ex-husband—and only as David's father?

"Shall we call Grace?" Paxton repeated.

The man was right. A good lawyer was something she really could use. She'd hired the best she could afford for the divorce and custody issues, but she was never fully convinced that the attorney had done all he could for them. As much as she believed that David deserved a father, she truly felt that with all of Ed's issues, David would be better off not knowing the man than having to learn for himself what a jerk his dad was. The truck turned up her mother's street and then shortly after, pulled into the driveway.

"I'll call Grace tomorrow morning." She reached for the handle as the truck came to a stop. Even though Ed had only texted her twice, she couldn't shake the feeling that things were about to get way more complicated than she wanted. With David about to go to bed and her mother in the habit of going to sleep early, the thought of sitting home alone stewing over Ed held little appeal. "Want to come in for some coffee or tea?"

"Would love to." Paxton threw the truck into park and climbed out. He'd barely had time to put both feet on the ground when the front door flew open and an excited David came running down the front steps.

To her surprise, Paxton was braced and ready when David flew into his arms. "I knew you'd come home with Mommy."

"And here I am. But in your pajamas, shouldn't you be inside."

The child looked momentarily contrite, nodded, and then with a grin as wide as the Rio Grande, looked Paxton in the eye. "You'll carry me inside, won't you?"

"You got it, sport." In a split second, as if Paxton had done the maneuver many times before, he shifted David around and had him hanging on piggyback style. "Here we go."

David cackled with delight as Paxton, pretending to be a horse, trotted them up the stairs and into the house.

"You can set him down, now." Sandra wanted to sound more stern, but couldn't stop smiling herself at how much fun both the boys in her life seemed to be having.

"To my room!" David shouted with the authority of an heir to a royal throne.

"Your wish is my command." Paxton hiked him higher on his back.

"Wait. You can't trot him up a flight of stairs." She set her hand on his arm, about to give David a short lecture on not taking advantage of people's kindness and how life isn't all fun and games and who knew what else when grinning as wide as her son, Paxton tilted his head to face her.

"Sure we can." With a wink and a "Last one to the top is a rotten egg," Paxton hurried up the steps, Sandra and her mother on his heels.

Following the direction of David's extended arm, Paxton trotted into the bedroom the boy shared with his mother and grandmother and dramatically dropped him on the small bed, collapsing beside him, feigning exhaustion.

"That was fun. Can we do it again?" David practically crawled over Paxton sprawled across the narrow bed.

"Another day," Sandra spoke up before Paxton agreed to more fun and games.

"You heard your Mom, sport." Paxton pushed to his feet and took a step back.

That disappointed look that didn't quite reach the level of a pout, almost had Sandra changing her mind, when David nodded quickly and once again smiling, faced Paxton. "Will you read my bedtime story to me?"

"Sure can." Paxton looked to the night table and the books piled high. He flipped through a few and turning to her asked, "Do you not have any chapter books?"

As much as she hated it, she had to shake her head. All they'd brought from home was what fit in her car and they'd never had a lot of extra money for new books.

Paxton's eyes danced with an idea as he leveled his gaze with her. "Didn't your dad read a lot of Louie L'Amour?"

"He loved those books." Her father reading to her as a little girl from his favorite books brought back warm memories.

"All in hardback. I still have them." Her mother bobbed her head sharply and snapped her fingers. "That's a great idea, I'll be right back."

A few moments later, David was tucked under the covers, had said his prayers with Paxton, and was now listening to the man read the first chapters of an old western. It didn't take long for her son to drift off to sleep.

Paxton pulled a receipt out of his pocket, stuck it on the pages he was reading, and closed the book. "That's why I thought prayers first. We always fell asleep when Mom or Dad read to us."

"Thank you. I could tell he really loved listening."

"These are not exactly children's books, but they're good clean fun and will do wonders for building his vocabulary."

"Like I said, thank you."

He nodded and handed her the book. "If it's all right with you, I'd be happy to come by tomorrow night and read the next chapter or two?"

And once again, her heart did that little flutter thing it did so often around Paxton. That the man showed so much interest in her son, more than his own father, was enough to make her cry. How blessed was she to have a man like this in her life. *In her life.* She had no idea what the future held for her, or Paxton, or her son, but right about now, she'd pay big bucks for this moment in time to never end. And wasn't that silly wishful thinking?

CHAPTER EIGHTEEN

Almost a week had gone by since Paxton and Sandra had met with his cousins Grace and Declan after she'd received her ex's text. The thing that Paxton couldn't figure out was why—despite Sandra having responded that she'd make arrangements for a visitation—David's father had yet to respond.

All Paxton could figure was that the man was a bigger jerk than what even Sandra had described. Having spent every night after finishing up at the job site working with David on his baseball, then joining the family for dinner, and finally tucking David in and reading to him, all Paxton knew is that Ed had been given the gift of a wonderful family and the guy had foolishly discarded it as easily as yesterday's trash.

"How deep you planning on digging that hole?" Glaring at the hole in the corner by the front porch, Quinn sighed.

Pulling his mind back from his thoughts of David and Sandra and her jerk of an ex, Paxton glanced down at the hole he'd been digging for the Chinese Fringe flower shrub. So distracted by his thoughts, he'd dug a hole big enough to transplant a small tree. "Thinking about putting a Japanese Maple here instead."

Quinn lifted one eyebrow at his brother. "Right." His brother shook his head. "Planning on selling beachfront real estate in Vegas too?"

Busted. Why did he bother trying to hide things from his siblings? They all knew each other too well. Even though the special connection that everyone had noted was heightened between him and his twin Owen, they could all read each other like a proverbial book. "Digging helps clear the mind."

"You keep up this kind of digging and you won't have a mind left to clear."

"Ha, ha." He flashed a forced smile.

"Seriously, dude. You're not going to be able to fix anything by messing up your lady's landscape."

"She's not *my* lady." Not that he wouldn't love that, but his gut had told him that Sandra needed him to take things slow. Even though some days it killed him, slow and steady was his plan.

"Right."

"She's not."

"Fine. She's not. But that doesn't change things. Stop overthinking and over digging." Quinn stepped in closer. "Listen, it's going to be okay. Declan and Grace are on top of all this. If the lady matters to you, then she matters to the whole family. We all have both your backs."

"I know." Resting his hands on the top of the shovel handle, Paxton nodded. "I appreciate it."

Quinn pulled the shovel out from under him. "You go get the plants out of the truck. I'd better do the digging."

A smile tugged at his cheeks. Of all his siblings, Quinn was the Sour Patch Kid. At first sour on the outside then sweet and chewy on the inside. No matter his expression, or gruffness, the whole family knew that Quinn had a heart of gold and would be the first one at their side in a moment of need.

With his brother's help, Paxton had the two Fringe flowers anchoring the edges of the front porch planted, and now he was ready for the Dwarf Nandinas to line the front.

"Well, isn't this a sight to see." Ryan stood in the front walkway with his hands on his hips, his gaze darting from the newly planted shrub to Quinn. "How much did Pax have to pay you to pick up the shovel?"

Not easily goaded, Quinn merely rolled his eyes at their brother. "Quit yakking and grab the wheel barrow. There's more to plant here and I bet Sandra would be really happy to see the front of her house done when she pops by later today."

"Oh." All teasing expressions washed away, and without another question, Ryan turned on his heel and searched for the wheel barrow. "Give me two minutes to let the guys inside know I'm shifting gears. Be right back."

And just like that, Ryan was now doing exactly as Quinn had said. Because Sandra mattered to him, she mattered to them. No questions asked, if this was for Sandra, to make her happy, then his carpenter brother would roll up his sleeves and play with the dirt.

By the end of the morning, they had all the shrubs planted and Paxton was pouring mulch when he heard a small gasp. Straightening to his full height, he turned to see Sandra standing on the sidewalk, her eyes circled round and her hand on her mouth.

"It's beautiful," she muttered through spread fingers still covering her mouth. "I knew we were getting close, but didn't realize it was this close."

Shrugging one shoulder, he took a step closer to her. "I would still be digging holes if my brothers had not pitched in to help."

"Doesn't matter who did it. It all looks so lovely." She swallowed hard. "And homey. Reminds me of the house I grew up in."

He hadn't given it any thought, but she was right. The traditional craftsman-like front of the small house was indeed very similar to the larger home she'd grown up in. Though he didn't really remember the landscaping much.

Slowly moving forward, she looked at the angle and spacing of the Nandinas. More depth closer to the walkway and narrowing to a single shrub in the far corner before what would someday be a lovely burst of color from the full-grown Fringe flowers. "I can't find the words."

"No words needed. Your face says it all."

She whipped around to face him and threw her arms around him for too-brief a moment before stepping away. "This is so much more than I ever imagined."

"Glad you like it."

"I love it." She slapped her hands together excitedly. "Wait till David sees this."

Not wanting to burst the joy of the moment, Paxton debated if he should ask if she'd heard from Ed. Looking at how her eyes sparkled and lips tipped up in a sweet smile, he opted to let it slide. If the jerk ever reached out to her again, she'd tell Paxton. At least he sure hoped so.

With every passing week, the house was looking more and more like a home. Inside, the raw cabinets in the kitchen had been installed. The next day the bathroom vanities had gone in. When the cabinets got painted and the countertops installed a few days ago, she couldn't believe her eyes. But even the tiniest of apartments, when updated to television renovations show standards, was still an apartment. This, the plants and shrubs, the dirt and mulch, all surrounding a front porch, this screamed happy home. "I just can't believe it."

"Pretty soon you'll get a key and it will be all yours." Paxton stood grinning at her.

"Like I said, it's almost too good to believe."

"Then maybe I shouldn't show you what we did in the back."

Her jaw dropped and her eyes opened wide and her voice simply wouldn't come. Instead, she merely nodded.

Paxton extended his hand to her and she happily threaded her fingers in his. Life simply couldn't get any better than this. Well, she felt her cheeks heat, maybe life could get just a little better.

The screen door to the back porch slammed shut behind them and Paxton waved to the right. Hanging from the rafters, a solid wood swing hung.

"Ryan made it. He said every porch needs a swing."

"I love it! How perfect. Ryan is a sweetheart." Still holding onto his hand, she walked over and sat in the swing, tugging him to sit beside her.

With a shove of his foot, Paxton set them to rocking.

"This is amazing. From here I can watch David play on

the porch or in the yard."

"That's the idea." Paxton nodded. "We considered hanging it against the wall, but then you'd only see the yard. By putting it here at the end, you have a fuller view."

"A perfect view." Heaving out a contented sigh, she pushed to her feet. "I could sit all day, but tonight is Girls' Night and I'm invited."

"Oh." Paxton's smile slipped. "Where?"

"At Nora and Neil's. They still live in the apartment over the clinic and Nora's kicking your brother out for the night."

Chuckling loudly, Paxton bobbed his head. "That would explain why Aunt Eileen was cooking so early this morning."

"Yep. She's expecting a crowd of Farraday men for dinner and time killing." Wishing she could stay a little longer, she let go of Paxton's hand and stood. "It's such a pretty afternoon, I'm going to walk over. See you tomorrow?"

He nodded. "Tomorrow, but I can drive you over."

"Nah. I've been eating too many homemade desserts. The walk will do me good."

Slowly, she walked through the house, taking her time, looking at the pretty light wood flooring. For so long dark was popular but she really preferred the brightness of the lighter floors.

As she walked, she pondered the rooms, where to put furniture, what kind of pieces she'd need. How she'd decorate David's room. Maybe find him a race car bed at a garage sale. Would be worth driving to Butler Springs for a good deal. Halfway to Nora's, a horn tooted. Not till it tooted again did she think to look.

Grace had slowed and was easing up Main Street with the passenger window down. "Heading to Nora's?"

"Yep."

"Hop in. I'll give you a ride."

The few blocks left were no big deal, but she grinned at her old friend and climbed in. "Thanks."

"I heard that Toni is bringing her cake balls. That means

tomorrow you may want to walk everywhere twice."

Sandra kicked her head back laughing. "That good?"

"Oh, yeah."

The fun thing about longtime childhood friends was that no matter how much time passed, once they got together it was as if no time at all had gone by. They were still laughing merrily after Grace parked and they climbed the stairs to the apartment over the veterinary clinic.

"I heard them talking about moving to a real house." Grace carried a bottle of wine. "I think that's family code for their thinking of starting a family. Which will set Aunt Mariah off. That woman has a burr in her butt when it comes to Texas."

Paxton had shared a little of the family rift, though he and his brothers didn't really understand what it was all about. From inside, she could hear the ladies laughing. "Sounds like they're having a good time already."

"Always." Grace had her hand on the doorknob at the top of the stairs when Sandra's phone pinged.

Expecting it to be Paxton with some silly last-minute words of advice, her heart sank to her feet when the text from Ed came across her screen.

"What's wrong?" Grace froze in place. "You're as white as a sheet."

Sandra couldn't bring herself to read the text out loud; instead she handed Grace the phone.

"I see what you mean." Grace read each word, her mouth twisting tightly as she reached the end. "So he's coming next weekend."

"That's what he says now."

"What you're telling me is he could change his mind?"

"Or forget. If he's drunk now, which would explain the expletives, he might not even remember he told me he'd be here to see David next Saturday."

"If there's a God in heaven, he'll not only forget what he said, he'll forget all about you two and fade away."

"Not going to happen any time soon." Drawing in a deep breath and blowing it out slowly, she slipped the phone into her purse and plastered on her best effort at a smile. "Shall we go inside and forget all about Ed Morton?"

"Sounds good to me. But," Grace lightly rested her hand on Sandra's shoulder, "whenever the jackass shows up, we'll all be ready."

That much Sandra Lynn understood, and was damn thankful for.

CHAPTER NINETEEN

The plans had been made. As much as Paxton had hoped that Ed Morton would simply ride off into the horizon and never return, the man had indeed reached out to Sandra Lynn more than once to confirm he was coming Saturday. The one thing that had struck Paxton as incredibly telling, was that most kids loved their parents no matter their flaws. When a parent was a workaholic, or just indifferent, their kids never stopped hoping for precious one-on-one time. They always forgave and always hoped and always expected the next time to be different, better.

Not David. He didn't react much either way when Sandra finally told him yesterday that his father was coming to visit Tuckers Bluff. The only thing David had asked was if she and Paxton would be there too.

Sandra had been fussing over her son as if he were full grown and heading off to war. She'd straightened his clothes, brushed stray strands of hair off his forehead, gave him an ice cream snack, kissed his forehead, brushed his hair some more and kissed him again. If Paxton didn't feel the same unease at letting this sweet boy hang out with his idiot of a father, he would have found her behavior amusing.

"Can I have a grilled cheese sandwich?" David sat at the kitchen table. "I'm hungry."

"Oh sweetie." Again, Sandra Lynn brushed his hair and kissed his temple. "You're going to have lunch with Daddy at the café."

"Do they make grilled cheese?"

Paxton moved to stand beside the young boy and placed

his hand on his shoulder. "I'm sure Frank can fix anything you like."

"Okay." The boy grinned up at him and Paxton actually wondered how much trouble would they be in if he just took the kid to spend the day anywhere but in Tuckers Bluff.

"I don't know." Sandra stood by Paxton's side, watching her son wash his hands at the kitchen sink. "I wish I could join them."

"I know, but Grace explained how it's key you let the man have time with just David so that you're not in breach of the custody agreement."

"I still don't have to like it."

"No. None of us do, but we've got this covered. You're not alone."

Her gaze shifted to his and despite the concern oozing from her every movement, her eyes momentarily softened and she smiled at him. "That's the best thing you could have said to me. I've been doing this alone for so long."

His heart twisted. "No matter what, you can always count on me." He came within inches of telling her that he loved her, and if she'd let him, would happily take care of her and David for the rest of their lives.

"Thank you." She blew out a deep sigh. "All right, David. Time to go see your father."

Without a word, the child hopped off the short step stool and hurried to his mother's side. "Are we going to ride in your truck?"

"We are." Paxton smiled at him.

"When I grow up I want a truck too." David walked out the front door and Paxton prayed that today went better than anyone expected.

It only took a few minutes to drive over to the café. A public location was part of the deal that Ed and Sandra had agreed on. The truck parked, they strolled into the café the same as any other day. The difference this afternoon was a disgruntled customer shouting at one of the waitresses. "Road kill would taste better than this garbage."

At his side Sandra stiffened, and there was no reason for Paxton to ask who was making a scene.

"Sorry, sir." The waitress retrieved the plate and opened her mouth for another apology, just as Abbie walked up, smiled at the young girl, and sent her back to the kitchen.

"I apologize if the food wasn't up to your expectations." Abbie didn't bother to smile, she didn't have to be a mind reader to know that it would be wasted on the irate customer.

"Stupid place doesn't even serve beer. What kind of restaurant doesn't serve booze."

"We don't." Abbie didn't even flinch. "Perhaps you might want to try O'Faredeigh's. Their food and spirits might be more to your liking."

"Can't. Waiting on someone."

Abbie looked up and her gaze met her husband's sitting at the counter next to his cousin Grace.

Pushing to her feet, Grace nodded at Declan who'd been standing by the front door. Together the two walked over to Sandra. Grace took David's hand. "Shall we go see your dad?"

David looked up at Paxton and his heart squeezed. How could Ed be such an asshat.

"It's okay. Your mom and I will be at another table."

That seemed to make the boy feel a little better.

The sight of Declan in uniform seemed to flip a switch in Ed. His gaze landed on David and for a fraction of a second, Paxton thought the man might smile. Maybe things would be okay.

In the opposite corner of the café, Paxton opted to sit beside Sandra instead of across from her. Their backs to the window, they could easily see everything happening at Ed and David's table, even if they couldn't hear. Of course, Declan and Grace were seated at the table directly next to Ed and David. Later, Paxton would ask them about the conversation between father and son.

They ordered something to eat, and carefully watching the table across the way, barely touched their food. At one point, David must have said something Ed didn't like, because he grabbed his son's arm, hard. Sandra gasped, Paxton bit down hard, Declan pushed his chair back, and thankfully, Ed let go and this time did smile.

The only comforting thing at the moment was that scattered around the diner, several other chairs scraped along the floor at that moment. Adam had actually gotten to his feet, his wife tugging at his arm to sit. Paxton knew exactly how his cousin felt. Sitting still, only able to watch, was killing him. Something needed to be done about Ed Morton.

"Is this day ever going to end?" Sandra kept her gaze on her son. Time was crawling by at the pace of a sick snail.

Part of Paxton wanted Ed to try something, anything, that they could use against him to keep him away from David. The smarter side of him knew that it was in David's best interest for Ed to walk the straight and narrow with this visit. If only Paxton had the wisdom of Solomon.

"Do you smell something?" Sandra sniffed at the air. "Do you think Frank is burning someone's lunch?"

To Paxton the sour smell didn't seem like burned food. Glancing around, he looked for anything out of the ordinary. Another few minutes passed and the smell grew stronger. Declan must have noticed the same thing as he was on his feet, walking toward the back of the café. When he reached the restrooms, he looked left then right. Just as he looked up, a loud pitch siren sounded. Someone shouted, "Fire!" and in a flash, chairs scraped across the tile floor, hushed murmurs tinged with panic filtered through the café. Another moment and the overhead sprinklers went off, showering everyone with water. The controlled panic instantly slid into total chaos as people pushed away from tables, slid out of booths, and slammed into each other in a race for the front door. Everyone except for Ed and David. Neither was anywhere to be seen.

Even though Declan had been sitting near Ed and David, and Grace had been at their side as well, the moment the alarm sounded and Sandra lost sight of her son, panic coursed through every drop of blood in her body. Her baby. "Where is he?"

"I don't see him." Paxton's hand landed on her lower back as he maneuvered her through the sudden rush of movement and the increasing smoke filling the café. "We'll find him."

Immediately, Paxton's phone pinged a message. "Grace lost contact."

Another ping, this time from Adam. "Not near me and Meg."

The phone began sounding off with message after message. So intent on watching David with his father, Sandra hadn't noticed all the Farradays scattered around the diner. One by one they pinged back and forth. Aunt Eileen and the social club had been seated near the door and were now spreading out along Main Street. How had she not seen Brooks and his wife in the diner, or Connor and Catherine in the side parking lot?

Nora and Neil had been by the rear kitchen door. "No sign of anyone in the back."

"Where is he?" She didn't want to sound like a crazed frantic parent, but any second now she was about to lose her mind. "How far can Ed get with him?"

"Not very." Finally, out the front door, the street was blocked with fire trucks and police cars. Standing by Connor, Paxton looked up and down the street. "Reed was watching his car."

"He was?" She didn't even know what kind of car her ex drove now, how did everyone else know?

"We have a reading on their location." Paxton stared at his phone.

"Reading?" Now Sandra felt totally confused.

Paxton nodded, still looking down at the phone. "I put a tracker in his backpack. The police are monitoring it."

"Why did you do that?" The words had barely left her lips when she realized what a stupid question that was. Paxton was no idiot. Of course he'd realized her ex was not to be trusted. "Never mind. Thank you."

"Would love to take credit for it, but it was Declan's

idea. I just helped with the logistics." He stared at the screen a few more moments, then looked up at the café. "The fire was set in the trash can in the ladies' room."

"The ladies room? But I never saw Ed get up, never mind go into the ladies' room." This made no sense to her. "Do you think the fire has nothing to do with Ed?"

"Not on your life." He grabbed her hand. "Come on. The backpack is just up the street."

He didn't have to ask her twice. Threading her fingers with his, she trotted to keep up with his long strides. Two shops up, he turned the corner and led her to the back alley. His gaze scanning the length of the space, a deep frown settled between his brows as Esther, the police dispatcher, came up to a nearby trash can.

Like a magician pulling a rabbit out of the hat, Esther pulled David's backpack out of the trash can. "For an idiot, he had the good sense to ditch the tracker."

"Assuming he knew there was a tracker." Paxton sighed and looked intently down the alley. "He won't get far."

More than anything, Sandra hoped he was right.

Just turning onto Main Street again, Sister from the boutique came hurrying up to them, panting heavily and frantically waving her arm. "He's heading up Pearl Street. Sissy spotted him through the window. Took us another moment to realize the little boy he was dragging along was David. That nasty man, I knew he was nothing but trouble the day he came shopping."

"Did you tell Declan?" Paxton rocked on his heels, clearly ready to go running after the man himself.

Sister bobbed her head. "Sissy runs faster than I do. It's those long, skinny legs."

"Runs?" Paxton's eyes widened and Sandra's breath caught. Surely that sweet older woman wasn't chasing Ed?

Her hands on her knees and her breath coming in short and fast gulps, Sister nodded. "We had to do something. I called Declan, but couldn't keep up so I came looking for you."

Good grief, Sissy was chasing after her ex. Suddenly having everyone and their grandmother in your business

was the sweetest blessing Sandra had ever known. Everyone
had her back, but if anything happened to Sissy because so
many years ago Sandra was stupid enough to marry Ed,
she'd never forgive herself.

Paxton's phone dinged again, and turning to Sandra, he
grabbed her arm. "Someone needs to get Sister to the police
station. I'd rather join the hunt for Ed."

"There's something else you should know." The plump
blonde was still desperately trying to catch her breath.
"There's a woman with him."

That would certainly explain the fire in the ladies'
room.

"She drives a two-door sports car."

"How do you know that?" The question escaped
Sandra's lips before her filter had a chance to kick in. So
what if the Sisters knew more about her ex, his girlfriend,
and their car than she did? All that mattered now was
getting any information from anyone that would bring her
baby boy home… and soon.

CHAPTER TWENTY

"She came into the shop yesterday." Sister shook her head, peering over Sandra's shoulder, keeping an eye on the happenings up the street. "We saw her get into that little sports car. Usually it's the men in the flashy sports cars, so we thought it interesting."

Paxton listened carefully to every word the shopkeeper had to say, all the time keeping his attention on the cell phone and messages going back and forth. "Oh for the love of..."

"What?"

Heaving a heavy sigh, Paxton looked up at Sandra. "According to Declan, Ned saw Sissy running up the street past his shop and now he's in on the chase too."

"Chase?"

"When Sister catches her breath, could you please take her to the police station? I'm going to go see for myself what the heck is going on."

"Nonsense." Sister frowned. "You two go. I can find my own way back. I'm sure by now they've caught up with him and everyone is back where they belong."

He smiled sweetly at the older woman, already knowing that was not the plan. Declan had suspected something like this would happen. He'd had too much experience with similar situations when he worked in Dallas. What his plan didn't need was every member of the community getting in on the action.

Her gaze darting from Paxton to Sister, Sandra seemed torn.

"It's up to you," he told her softly.

With a single dip of her chin, she straightened her

shoulders. "I'm coming with you. And when we reach David, I'm giving him the biggest hug any child or adult ever had."

"Atta girl." Sister grinned up at her. "Go."

Taking hold of her hand, he hurried back to where their car was parked. Based on the texts bouncing back and forth, he opted to head to the end of town. Sure enough, Adam was in his truck, pulling the door shut moments before taking off. Brooks was doing the same thing from across the street.

Another minute and Connor's voice could be heard over a walkie-talkie that Declan held. "I can see his tail lights. Idiot has no idea."

Sandra frowned. "No idea of what?"

"Ten four." Declan spoke into the mic. "Adam and Brooks are heading that way. I'm pulling Morgan and Finn off their positions and sending them to cover any possible alternate routes."

"What's he talking about?" Sandra asked.

"We've had folks stationed at both egresses out of town. We didn't know where he was going to try and go with David."

"You knew he was going to take him?"

Paxton shrugged. "Didn't know, but suspected."

She bobbed her head and still frowning, turned to face Declan.

"Looks like Oklahoma is the winner." Declan looked at his watch. "Reed is already positioned about five miles ahead of Morton.

Another voice cut in. Esther, the police dispatcher was back on the job. "I've alerted the Oklahoma State Police. King was waiting for your call. He's ready to be wherever we tell him."

Staring intently at Declan and Jamison standing over the hood of a car with a map open, Sandra's grip on his hand tightened. "I don't understand. If they know where Ed is, why aren't they stopping him?"

Just as he opened his mouth to speak, Ian's voice came over the walkie-talkie. "In position. GPS is still tracking."

Sandra's eyes rounded. "How many people are in on this?"

Despite the seriousness of the situation, Paxton couldn't help but find her reaction a tiny bit humorous. "A lot."

"Your brothers are in on this too, aren't they?"

He nodded. "They're on alternate routes. Just in case Ed veers off the highway."

"All right. Back to my original question. Why aren't they stopping him now?"

This entire situation was insane. Sandra had no idea who the woman with Ed was, but she suspected, if the gal drove a fancy sports car, she had to have money because the Ed she'd been married to couldn't afford a tricycle. And why the heck was half the town and pretty much every Farraday chasing after her ex?

"Kidnapping is a serious offense. Kidnapping and crossing the state line is a federal offense."

Understanding dawned. "They're setting him up for a bigger fall."

Paxton bobbed his head.

"And there will be plenty of witnesses."

Again, the man she'd grown to care about, whether she wanted to or not, nodded.

"You two going to stand there gabbing all day or are you going to be in on the bus?"

Turning his wrist to see the time, Paxton shook his head. "He's gotten over an hour head start on us—"

"One hour and twelve minutes to be precise." Declan cut his brother off.

"We'll never make it."

For the first time since they'd arrived, Declan actually smiled. "Ethan's in the helo. He's been casually tracking their position and keeping us one step ahead of them. He should be landing any minute."

As if summoned, the sound of a helicopter whirling

above sounded loud and clear. What Sandra had no idea about, was where the heck was the guy going to land? Another few minutes and her question was answered as the helicopter descended several houses away.

Again, Declan smiled. "Old man Navarette has the biggest yard in the neighborhood. When we asked permission to land, the guy lit up as if I'd told him he'd won the lottery."

Without another word, Paxton took hold of her hand and hurried them up the block.

"Is this how they've been tracking him? With Ethan? Isn't it risky to pull him away from the chase?"

"Ethan is insurance. While everyone was in the café, Declan had his deputy, Reed, place a tracking device under the sports car's front fender. The thing Ed forgot is that in a small town, it's one thing to pop into town for a few days and spy on your ex, but if you return in a new flashy car, it will only take the town a few minutes to know."

"You two ready for the show?" Unlike everyone else's serious expressions, Ethan had a knowing grin on his face. Had to be the military background.

How did all these people stay so calm? Had the situation not been so dire, Sandra would have found the helicopter ride fascinating. As it was, she just wished they could go faster.

"You okay?" Paxton squeezed her hand.

"Ask me an easier question." She tried to put on a brave smile, but she had a lot to learn about the Farraday confidence.

"It's going to be okay."

That's what she kept telling herself. Every few minutes another memory of her summers at the ranch, when Adam shot the head off a rattle snake that was seriously too close to where they'd been horsing around, the time she slipped in the creek and Neil and Owen had strung a rope across the area and Paxton had dangled from his knees to catch her as she floated by, and so many others. There wasn't anyone she would trust more with her son than Paxton and his family.

"And let the show begin." Paxton pointed to the road below them.

Sirens were blaring, lights were flashing, and Ed was flying so fast Sandra bit down on her lower lip, worrying about her son at the hands of his lunatic father. Just ahead, Ed couldn't see what she and Paxton could—a line of cars across the border, police cars waiting to nab him. Relief washed over her. She didn't want that man having anything to do with her sweet boy.

"Guy is driving right into the waiting arms of police officials in two states. Lucky guy." Ethan's sarcasm was almost amusing… almost.

Just as Ed crossed the state line, and spotted his reception committee, he gunned it, racing even faster, clearly determined to plow through the barricade. Sandra's heart skipped a beat, her grip on Paxton tightened, and before she could swallow and say a prayer, one by one Ed's tires blew out and his car fishtailed but stopped right in the hands of the Oklahoma police, and most likely if Ian was there, the Texas Rangers.

The helo landed slightly back from the action. No point in blowing everyone about. Or giving Ed an opportunity to run on foot. Out of the helicopter, still holding on to Paxton's hand, Sandra ran as fast as she could toward the commotion. Seeing Ed with his hands handcuffed behind him gave Sandra pause. Was that what she wanted?

The shrill sound of "Mommy" snapped her out of her moment of guilt. Ed Morton had made his own bed. Nothing that happened to him now was Sandra's fault. Before she could squat to her son's level, David flung himself at her. If not for Paxton holding her steady, her son would have easily knocked her over.

"I love you, Sweetie." Sandra's arms had never wrapped tighter around her son. Practically rocking him as she swayed from side to side, looking over his little shoulder, she faced Paxton and mouthed, *Thank you.*

CHAPTER TWENTY-ONE

This Saturday had been a long time coming. Paxton had wanted to get a family baseball game together for the kids since he'd first learned of David's interest in the sport. Since last week's insane escapade with David's father, the kid had been unusually quiet and even withdrawn. Having a normal, fun-filled family game seamed more important than ever.

"Did you take the bases outside?" Aunt Eileen stood in the middle of the kitchen, waving a large spoon around as she mixed the biggest bowl of mustard potato and egg salad he'd ever seen.

"Done." His arms full carrying a massive tray of marinated ribs for the grill, Uncle Sean nodded at his wife. "And Finn checked the diamond lines from yesterday. Still visible and ready for the game."

"And the bleachers?" His aunt returned the spoon to the bowl and continued blending.

"Done as well." Connor slapped his hat against his leg and stomped his boots at the back door mat. "Also set up the west field for a little horseplay later on if the kids aren't too tired."

Aunt Eileen lifted her gaze from the bowl, paused, then turned to her nephew. "Wouldn't tired kids be an oxymoron?"

A burst of laughter filled the room. The only person in the room at the moment with children, Connor managed to mumble through his mirth. "Good point."

"I still think painting the lines on the field was a bit over the top." Paxton hadn't meant for the game to be such a production, but it shouldn't surprise him that when his aunt heard of his plans, she'd go all out to make the day a huge event for family and friends. Once the game would be over, there'd be food and music, and knowing his aunt, there'd be dancing too.

The front door flew open, and carrying a large duffle in each hand, Quinn stomped into the house.

"Were you raised in a barn?" Aunt Eileen called from the kitchen. "Close the door."

Quinn shook his head. "Sorry, but Sandra Lynn and David are—"

"Right behind him." Sandra Lynn yanked her son's cap off his head.

Anyone who had ever spent any length of time at the Farraday ranch knew that one of Aunt Eileen's pet peeves was wearing hats in the house. Especially baseball caps, she would not hesitate to point out to her family and their friends that there was no sunshine in the living room.

A bit more clingy than usual this last week, David was pressed up against his mother.

"The kids are all out in the backyard." Aunt Eileen stepped back and reached for a different plate. "If you go tell them to wash their hands, everyone can have one freshly baked chocolate chip cookie before the game starts."

David's eyes lit up and without any of the hesitation he'd shown all week, the kid sprinted through the house and out the back door.

"Cookies gets 'em every time." Aunt Eileen smiled after the boy. "Good thing I baked extra this morning."

With no one watching, Paxton stole a quick kiss and taking Sandra Lynn's hand, squeezed it tightly in his.

Smiling up at him, she squeezed his hand back then turned to the kitchen. "I'll have to remember that trick."

"'Fraid not." With a grin as wide as the house, his aunt smiled back at Sandra. "Only works for grandmothers and pseudo-grandmothers. You parents are stuck with rules."

Another minute of chuckling and teasing about child rearing versus grandparenting and the door bumped open again. This time Declan and his family came in the door. The youngest of the Farraday grands, Declan's son Thomas wiggled right out of his mother's arms and toddled like only a fourteen-month-old could across the room, repeating PawPaw until his grandfather scooped him up and sliding him onto his shoulders, carried the gleeful child outside with the others.

"I do miss that age." Sandra's gaze lingered momentarily on the door that slammed shut behind Uncle Sean, so long that Paxton's mind was spinning.

"Since the kids are all outside, I thought y'all might like the latest news on Mr. Edward Morton."

"Good or bad?" Sandra asked so softly, that without thinking, Paxton curled her into his side and kissed her temple.

"Depends." Declan shrugged.

"On?" Paxton wished the man would just get to the point.

"Whose boots you're wearing. I'd say for us, it's a sweet catch. For Ed, not so much."

"All right." Paxton sighed. "Just spit it out."

"You know that sleek little sports job?"

Both he and Sandra nodded.

"Stolen."

Sandra's mouth dropped slightly open.

"We already knew that he'd be up on federal parental kidnapping charges the minute he crossed the state line which, based on the circumstances, should see him getting somewhere close to eight years on the low side. Long enough for David to grow up without a mean drunk standing over his shoulders."

Those words had Sandra Lynn stiffening. Squeezing her a moment, he kissed her temple again, pleased when she relaxed against him.

"But the *piece de resistance* that, my friends, I just learned about a few hours ago… The idiot has upgraded his drug of choice from booze to heroin, which he had in his possession. David is not going to have to deal with that man for a very, very long time."

Sandra sighed. "I don't know if I should feel sorry for Ed or kick my heels up and give a cheer."

"Today, I vote for cheer," Aunt Eileen called from the

kitchen. "Tomorrow we can feel bad for the jerk."

His aunt's perfect delivery had Sandra giggling. Bless that woman.

From where Sandra Lynn stood, the day could not have gone any better. There were so many Farraday grandkids running around similar to David's age. Adam's daughter Fiona, Connor's son Shane, Jamison's son Brandon, and Declan's daughter Caitlin were all within a few months of each other. Then, of course, Declan and Becky had the cutest little boy, Finn and his wife had a little girl similar in age to little Tommy, and Grace and her husband had a little girl a smidge younger than Tommy. How much fun for all those kids to have so many first cousins.

Not only were there plenty of kids David's age, but Connor's older daughter Stacy, and Brooks's daughter Helen, along with Ethan's daughter Brittany, were the coordinators of the kids' game. Splitting their friends with the younger brood, the games were pretty evenly matched and even the younger ones who, like David, had never had a lot of training or practice, did really well. It didn't hurt any that the older kids were cheering everyone on. This really was a crazy nice family.

Once the baseball game was over, as Connor had mentioned earlier, the kids still had plenty of energy, so they all moved to the side field where Connor had set things up for them to play mutton tag and grab the bandana off the lambs necks. Then there was the stuffed steer roping, and a slew of other games including the three-legged races. The kids were laughing so hard, but the best part was that David was running and playing and laughing with all the others. The quiet little boy of the last week after the ordeal with his father was gone and her happy boy was back.

"You're smiling." Paxton handed her a plastic cup with his aunt's fresh squeezed strawberry lemonade. "Care to share?"

"My son is happy."

Paxton slung an arm around her shoulder and followed her gaze to where David and the other children were playing some game akin to blind man's bluff. Grey and the other family dogs were also running about barking and bouncing and having as much fun as the kids. "He is."

"I owe it to you."

"I had little to do with it."

"You keep saying that, but without you, no one else would have gotten so involved."

"Of course they would have. Declan would have done the same regardless of me. After all, you were raised here too."

"All right." She sighed. "I'll give you that Declan is good and might have been able to anticipate Ed's intentions, but I have no doubts that they went the extra mile because you cared."

It took Paxton a long moment before he bobbed his head. "Let's settle at everyone cares."

"This may not be a good time, or the right place, but I can't help it. I love you, Paxton Farraday."

His smile dimmed slightly and if not for the intensity that grew in his eyes as he studied her, she would have sworn that she'd just ruined everything.

"I have to ask." He blew out a slow long breath. "Love me as in oh you're my best fishing buddy, or love me as in I don't want to ever live without you?"

"For the first time in my life I know what it feels like to be head over heels, honest-to-goodness, in love with a man."

"You'd better mean me, because I have been head over boot heels in love with you since you were eight years old."

At that very moment, someone handed his aunt a microphone and she tapped on it, getting everyone's attention. "So y'all know. Supper is ready. Ribs and fixings are on the back porch. As you've already found, the drinks are in coolers along the other side."

Applause sounded from all around. Just about every member of the Farraday clan was in attendance as well as half the town. Even Sister and Sissy had closed the shop to be here.

"Sing!" someone shouted from not far away.

Aunt Eileen shook her head. "Not tonight. This gathering is for the young ones."

Several more voices followed, "Sing!"

Paxton's aunt rolled her eyes. "Fellas, give a gal a break."

Now pretty much every adult and half the kids had their hands cupped around their mouths and were hollering good and loud, "Sing!"

"All right. All right." Aunt Eileen waved her hands at the crowd. "You win." She spun around, whispered something to her sister-in-law Ann, and then turned back to the family gathered around the wooden dance floor Aunt Eileen always had laid down when there was family and music. "This one is for all you lovebirds out there. One of my favorite songs by Old Blue Eyes."

It took Sandra a few moments to place the opening notes, but as soon as Paxton's aunt started crooning, *Some day, when I'm awfully low*, she recognized what had also been one of her dad's favorite oldies tune.

"Shall we?" Paxton raised her one hand and she knew that he'd been the one to ask his aunt to sing that song.

At her nod, he twirled her into the fold of his arms. For the remainder of the tune, she found herself melted against him, comforted by his thoughtfulness and his deep low voice serenading her right alongside his aunt. Every time he crooned *'cause I love you*, her toes tingled and her heart danced. No matter how long and hard the last few years had been, absolutely nothing was sweeter than this very moment.

When the peppy tune slowed, and Aunt Eileen glanced at her husband, her voice dropping to sing the last lines, *the way you look tonight*, Paxton pulled her tightly against him, dipped her ever so slightly, and lifting her back into his arms, kissed her hard, and strong, and sweet and lovingly. Yep. Life had never been better.

EPILOGUE

The ribbon cutting day for the new charity project in town had finally arrived. Everyone was bopping around with delight. So many happy smiling faces, Quinn Farraday couldn't help but smile along with them. At least a little.

There was just one tiny little glitch. Paxton had fallen head over boot heels in love with Sandra Lynn. That of itself wasn't a problem. Her getting affordable new housing to live in when Paxton had been carrying a ring around in his pocket for almost two weeks was a potential fly in the charity's ointment. After all, if Sandra Lynn said yes, she would no longer be a single mom in need of assistance.

"Has he said anything to you?" Ryan took one last look at the cleaned-up little house, making sure it was ready for the major photo op that would be happening in about one hour.

"Not a word. But he's barked several times if that counts." Quinn rolled his eyes. His slightly older brother was behaving like a surly teen.

"Shh. Here they are." Ryan took a step aside and noticed the camera crew coming up the walk. "Is this being filmed for the show?"

Quinn shrugged. "Heck if I know."

"Well, I can't imagine a worse time to have anything on film."

"Why is that?" Quinn figured half of what was filmed would land on the cutting room floor anyhow.

"Really? Our brother wants to marry the woman who is about to be gifted affordable—and if I do say so myself—beautiful housing that she may have to give back sooner than later, and you want that on film? On national television?"

"You have a point."

"No sh…"

"You *were* about to say something appropriate, weren't you?" Their aunt came in the door, grinning at her nephews. "You two always were cute when I caught you with your hands in the cookie jar. Now what's all this about?"

"The house." Ryan waved his arm.

"Y'all did a great job. I see the film crew is here."

Both brothers nodded.

"But where is Sandra Lynn?"

This time the Irish twins born a little more than eleven months apart shrugged.

"There they are." Aunt Eileen pointed to the backyard.

Through the kitchen plate glass window Sandra and David could be seen in the yard, Paxton walking alongside them.

"They are cute, aren't they?" Aunt Eileen had a sappy look on her face as she stared out the window.

"Cute wasn't the first word that came to mind." Quinn was thinking *sappy suckers* but cute would do.

"Look at that." Aunt Eileen pointed. "All three holding hands, David in the middle. They look like they've always been a family."

That they did. Quinn actually sighed. Surrounded by all his cousins with kids running after kids and his own brothers marrying one after the other, he really was starting to feel like he was missing out on something. At least a little.

"Oh, my." Aunt Eileen's eyes widened and her hands flew to her mouth.

Quinn whipped his head around to his brother outside in time to see him down on one knee holding a ring in front of David. "Ain't he supposed to be asking the girl to marry him?"

"That's the way it usually works," Ryan deadpanned.

"Men." Aunt Eileen shook her head. "He's asking David's permission. He's not wanting to just marry Sandra, he's marrying both of them."

"Oh," Ryan muttered.

"Makes sense," Quinn added. It actually made a whole lot of sense. Connor treated Stacy like his own daughter. As a matter of fact, the first time he'd met them he had no idea that she wasn't his daughter. So now, Paxton was about to do the same thing. Instant family. Maybe.

Another minute passed and David flung his arms around Paxton, almost knocking him over. Still gripping the ring box tightly in one hand, Paxton circled his other arm around David holding him steady, still on one knee, only now he was staring up at Sandra.

Quinn wasn't a romantic or a sap, but even he wished he could hear what the two were saying. Another second and Paxton's lips stopped moving while Sandra's head bobbed up and down so fast it was a wonder it hadn't fallen off.

"And there they go." Aunt Eileen laughed at all three tumbling to the ground, laughing and hugging and he was pretty sure Sandra Lynn was crying. "Oh. Here they come. Look busy."

"What?" Ryan asked.

"We don't want them to know we were spying on them." His aunt turned to fuss with non-existent dust on a perfectly clean kitchen counter.

"We weren't spying. We were looking. And if they didn't want us to see, then maybe my big brother should have proposed someplace more private." Quinn didn't mind turning his attention elsewhere, but he didn't like being called a spy.

The screen door squeaked open followed by the back door and Ryan muttered something about oiling the hinge before the ribbon cutting and disappeared.

Sandra Lynn stopped at the sight of Quinn and Aunt Eileen in the kitchen. "Oh, hi."

"Hello," was all either of them said, but his aunt had a grin on her face so wide that Sandra Lynn would have to be an idiot not to realize the cat was already out of the bag. Blushing, she didn't bother to hide her own grin. "You know?"

Aunt Eileen nodded.

"I guess I need to find the head of the charity." Sandra Lynn glanced down at her son, holding onto Paxton's hand. "It seems I don't need a house after all."

This time, staring at her as if she were an oasis in a dry desert, Paxton nodded. "I'm going to build her the perfect house—"

"I'm sorry," Quinn interrupted. "You?"

"Okay." His brother smiled at him. "We."

Quinn nodded. "As long as we're clear." Then it struck him, how much of an idiot was he. Turning to face Sandra he smiled, almost surprised to notice how much he felt like smiling. "Welcome to the family."

Spinning around, Sandra let go of Paxton's hand and threw her arms around Quinn for a quick hug and peck on the cheek. "Thank you. I always wanted a big family. Looks like dreams really do come true."

She took a step back against Paxton, who had not stopped grinning like the Cheshire Cat this entire time.

"Dreams most definitely come true." The way Paxton practically devoured the woman with his eyes actually made Quinn surprisingly uncomfortable.

Clearing his throat, Quinn extended his hand to David. "Why don't you help me find the charity guy for your mama to talk to?"

David eagerly accepted his hand and nodded yes.

"You too, old lady."

"Old?" He'd never seen his aunt's brows rise so high on her forehead before. "Better watch it."

Quinn couldn't help but chuckle. He really did love his aunt and uncle and the entire Farraday brood. "Let's, you know, leave them alone."

His aunt laughed. "In about fifteen minutes the place will be swarming, but yes, let's give them that."

Outside, his aunt had already cornered the charity reps. From what he could overhear from a distance, Paxton had given them a heads up that things might be changing and had actually lined up another local candidate. One of the waitresses at the café was also a single mother, struggling to build the American dream.

Glancing over his shoulder, he could see just a glimpse of Paxton and Sandra Lynn in a serious lip lock. Okay, maybe his aunt was right and they were indeed cute. And maybe he needed to stop drinking the water in this town before he found himself standing in front of a preacher and saying I do.

Shaking his head, he looked around at all the people he knew gathering for the ribbon-cutting ceremony. Every last one of his siblings and cousins looked more than happy, and yet, no matter how cute Paxton and Sandra looked, Quinn was absolutely not signing up to be next in line. Absolutely not.

MEET CHRIS

USA TODAY Bestselling Author of dozens of contemporary novels, including the award winning Aloha Series, Chris Keniston lives in suburban Dallas with her husband, two human children, and two canine children. Though she loves her puppies equally, she admits being especially attached to her German Shepherd rescue. After all, even dogs deserve a happily ever after.

More on Chris and all her books can be found at
www.chriskeniston.com

Follow Chris' Monday Blog at her website
ChrisKenistonAuthor

Follow Chris on Facebook at
ChrisKenistonAuthor

Never miss a New Release!
Sign up for News from Chris:
www.chriskeniston.com/newsletter.html

Questions? Comments?
I would love to hear from you! You can reach me at:
chris@chriskeniston.com

Milton Keynes UK
Ingram Content Group UK Ltd.
UKHW010821220424
441551UK00005B/392

9 798891 490154